# Wildflowers By The River

Diane E. Izzard

ISBN: 978-0-9970065-2-0

## *Dedication*

To Bob and Ruth who help open my mind to the possibilities.

## *Acknowledgements*

Many thanks to my family and friends for their help in completing this book.

Much appreciation to Debby Eye for performing the final edit. I am always grateful for her amazing talent and attention to detail.

Special thanks to the Conlee-Snyder Mural Committee for allowing the use of a portion of the Putnam County Wildflower mural for the cover.

Thanks to Shirley Bennett for her exceptional artistic talent in the painting of the Passion Flower.

# *One*

I awoke with a start and lie in bed holding my breath, listening for any sound. I heard the whirling sound of the ceiling fan above my bed as it went round and round. The cicadas roared outside my window in the dark and my golden retriever, Max, snored away at the foot of my bed. I sensed the presence of someone in the room with me. I didn't dare move. I didn't want whoever was there to realize I was awake. I smelled a musty odor like wet dirt. I strained my ears, lying perfectly still for what seemed like an eternity before convincing myself no one was there. I must have dreamed the noise that woke me I told myself. I took in a deep breath and started to breathe normally again, even though I was still aware of every noise around me. I looked at the clock, 3AM. I closed my eyes and tried to return to my blissful sleep, but instead I spent the next few hours tossing and turning, feeling unsettled.

I gave up trying to sleep at 6AM and got out of bed, to the delight of Max. I wanted to beat the summer oppressive humidity and heat in Florida and take Max for a walk before the temperature was unbearable. I pulled my long, unruly, dirty blond hair into a ponytail, dressed in shorts and a t-shirt, and my pink running shoes. I hurried down the hall to catch up with Max when I tripped over something sending me face down on the floor, with Max licking my face. I examined my bruised knees, brushed myself off, and looked to see the cause of my clumsiness. Two books were lying on the floor in front of the bookcase. That's strange, I thought as I bent over and picked up the books, glancing at the titles. They were books I had collected on the history of Palatka, Florida where I live and work. I wondered what made the books fall from the shelf. Max brought me out of my

1

trance, barking wildly, reminding me that he was waiting for his walk. I placed the books back on the shelf and rushed out the door with Max leading the way.

Our morning walks are always adventurous. The sounds of the many birds, from osprey to cardinals, fill the air celebrating the sunrise while the squirrels scurry around the large live oak trees lining the street. As we approached the parking lot to the public boat ramp, Max broke free to chase the seagulls sitting on the pavement watching the fishermen launch their boats. The birds took flight, to the delight of Max, barking at the sky.

"Hi Gus. How has the crabbing been lately?" Gus is a local fisherman and friend of my father's that I've known most of my life. He is like an uncle to me.

"With little rain so far this year the salt levels in the river are staying high and crabbing has been great. Did your Dad tell you about the whopper bass I caught the other night fishing with him?"

"Yes, he couldn't wait to rub it in. He told me I should have gone with you." My Dad owns a boat repair business and loves to fish. He bought me my first fishing pole as soon as I could walk. I go fishing with him every chance I get.

Max returned from clearing the parking lot of birds and barked impatiently at the fact that I was standing still and not walking. "Good luck today!" I yelled to Gus as Max and I resumed our brisk stroll. Max barked at every squirrel as they teased him persistently with their chattering noises. The breeze along the river felt heavenly on this warm, muggy morning. Max soon tuckered out from the heat and communing with all the animals. We slowly made our way back home so Max would not get overheated. By the time we reached the house Max was panting profusely and I was drenched in sweat and in need of a cool shower. I walked down the hall toward the bathroom, glancing at the books on the shelf, half expecting to see them on the floor again. All appeared normal and I laughed at myself for getting spooked.

I hurriedly showered and dressed so I wouldn't be late to open my store, Treasures and More. After I  graduated from college with a degree in Art History I was unable to find a job. Window shopping one day downtown I saw this quaint little shop with a Space for Rent sign in the window. I always loved old things and thought this would be a perfect space to sell unusual items I find at flea markets, garage sales, and estate auctions. My parents helped me with the down payment. My business has slowly grown as more tourists have been attracted to the quaint downtown area and away from the beaches and malls. I have a few regular customers who frequently stop by to see what treasures I've added to my collection.

The bell rang above the door of my store as I entered. I flipped the brightly lit green open sign on. I straightened the shelves and prepared the store for customers. Max curled up behind the register in his designated spot on an old red and gray hook rug I had found at a flea market. Max claimed it as his as soon as I had placed it on the floor. He quickly fell asleep after his fun packed morning and it was not long before his legs were twitching. He must be dreaming of chasing squirrels after being tormented by them during out morning stroll. I left Max to his dreams while I gently dusted the antique glass, jewelry, furniture, and unusual art I had collected. I fluffed the quilts hanging along the quilt rack. My quilter's club provides the quilts for me to sell. We meet once a week to quilt together and catch up on the latest events and gossip. They are forever trying to fix me up with some new guy they think is perfect for me. I haven't had much luck in that department. It seems like everyone I've ever dated only has one aspiration, to have enough money to buy a twelve pack of beer on the weekend and enough bait to go fishing. Now I am not saying those are horrible qualities to have in a man, I just wanted more.

I looked up as the bell over my door rang. "Good morning Gloria. You're in early today." Gloria works at the store on the weekends and two days a week. I met her during a garage sale excursion. Going to garage sales was a social event for Gloria. When I first met her she appeared to have stepped out of a beauty parlor with her steel gray hair curled tightly, finger nails and toe nails freshly painted, with a little make-up to add color to her face and lips, wearing a comfortable cotton skirt and sandals. She had a big smile on her face and a sparkle in her eyes as she happily greeted the people she ran into at the garages sales. After we met I told her about my store in conversation one day. She started stopping by the shop a couple of times a week just to visit and ask how I was doing. When I was busy with a customer she would patiently wait until I was free and keep me company. I soon realized she was the lonely one. Her husband had passed away a few months back and she didn't like sitting around the house all by herself. I offered Gloria a job since she spent so much time in my shop anyway, and I could use a break now and then. I explained that I couldn't pay her much, but if she wanted to help me out a couple of days a week it would be appreciated. Gloria was thrilled with the idea. She indicated she didn't need the money, but would enjoy helping around the store. She frequently comes in early and never hesitates to offer suggestions on where I can find more treasures for my store.

"How are you doing this morning, Maggie?" Gloria cheerfully announced as she walked into the store.

"To be honest, I'm dragging a little today. I didn't sleep much last night."

"Sorry to hear that. Are the creaks and groans of your new house keeping you awake?"

"You could say that." I recently purchased a home in the historical district a block from the St. Johns River. It was auctioned on the courthouse steps after its owners passed away. The property tax was not paid after the owners died, so the house was sold to pay the back taxes. I was surprised when I bid fifty-thousand dollars and no one bid higher than me. When the auctioneer yelled, "Sold for fifty-thousand dollars!" I just about fainted. I had been living with my parents since graduating from college and didn't really believe I could afford this rustic Victorian-style house. The bank had pre-approved a loan for sixty-thousand dollars, but I had to use my store as collateral. My enthusiasm quickly diminished when I walked into my new home. From the outside I could tell the home built in 1910 needed a fresh coat of paint. I hoped the inside was in better shape. The house had been neglected for several years. The air conditioning didn't work, so there was mold throughout the house, the two commodes wouldn't flush, the water coming from the faucet had a reddish tint, and some of the hardwood floors were rotten where the roof leaked around the three fireplaces. I've spent every waking hour during the last month slowly fixing up the house with the little amount of money I had. "It's funny you should mention strange noises in the house. Something woke me last night and this morning I found two books on the floor in front of the bookcase. They must have fallen off the shelf during the night. What would make books just fall from the shelf?"

"It was probably just a ghost!" Gloria teased.

"You're kidding, aren't you?" I asked.

"Well, I was until you started taking me seriously. There is a lot of history in this town. The Timucuan and Seminole Indians lived along the river before the Spanish took over. Then the British took the property from the Spanish and the Seminole tribe was driven from Palatka. There has been a lot of death from disease and war, as you know, in this area. I am sure there must be a few restless spirits in some of the older sections of town."

"Did you know the people that lived in the house before me?"

"If I remember correctly they moved here from up north some place. The husband worked at the wood processing plant. His wife kept pretty much to herself. They never had any children. The husband passed away several years ago. The wife seldom left the house. Our church tried to stop by to bring her some food and offer our assistance after her husband passed away, but she

5

would never answer the door. I just assumed she wanted to be left alone to grieve in private."

"How did she die?"

"One of her neighbors had become concerned when she noticed several days worth of newspapers still lying in the driveway. The neighbor contacted the police and they found the woman dead in her bed. It was rumored she had died of a heart attack."

"That's so sad. She must have been so lonely. To die with no one around who cared."

"The woman chose her fate. She didn't seem to want anyone in her life."

"Do you think her spirit could still be in the house?"

Before Gloria could answer, the bell above the door jingled. "Good morning Sylvia. What brings you by today?" Maggie asked.

"I need to buy a birthday gift for my mother in-law. I'm hoping you might have a suggestion for me."

"I just found this antique locket a week ago at an estate sale," I said as I opened the locket and handed it to her. "You could put a picture of her son or grandson inside for her to enjoy."

"That sounds like an excellent idea1 She would love that."

While I rang up the purchase, Gloria asked Sylvia, "How is everyone in your family doing?"

"My younger brother, Harper, just graduated with an environmental engineering degree and has accepted an offer to work for St. Johns River Management. He will be moving in with me until he can afford a place of his own."

"Is he married or dating anyone?"

"No, he's kind of shy and hasn't dated anyone seriously in a couple of years."

"You don't say. Did you hear that Maggie, an engineer with a good job?"

"Just stop. I don't need you finding me a date."

"When was the last time you had a date?"

"That's none of your business and I am sure when the time is right God will send the perfect man my way." To change the subject I asked Sylvia, "Are you coming to the quilting club Friday night?"

"Yes, I wouldn't miss it. I'll bring a batch of my double chocolate brownies."

"Yum! You know chocolate is my weakness," I told her.

"Got to run. Harper is coming in this afternoon with a car load of stuff from his dorm. I've got to clean out the guest room so he will have some place to put his things."

Sylvia raced out the door. "Now where were we?" Gloria asked. "Oh yes, I remember. We were talking about how long it has been since you had a date."

"Don't even go there. You're treating me like I am an old maid. I am only twenty-three years old and have many good years left. It's just a matter of time before my knight in shining armor comes and takes me away from all this." I laughed and swirled around, motioning to all my precious possessions around the store. Max woke from his nap and barked at the sound of my laughter. "It's all right boy, Gloria doesn't realize I already have the perfect boy in my life." I reached down and kissed Max on the nose. "You have loved me from the day I found you wandering on the street all smelly and dirty. You never complain about anything as long as you get walked and fed." Max licked me across the face as if he understood every word I said.

# *Two*

That evening while I painted the doors to my kitchen cabinets I thought about the woman that died in this house. Who was she? Why did she seldom leave the house? The history nut in me needed answers. After I finished painting for the evening I decided to check online to see what I could find. I searched the tax records and found the names Herman and Dorothy Evanston as the previous owners. I googled the name Dorothy Evanston and was surprised to see that she had been an artist. There were a few pieces of her art for sale by a prestigious art gallery in New York. That can't be right. Surely if there was a famous artist in town Gloria would have known about it. There were no more references to Dorothy Evanston online. Unable to keep my eyes open any longer, I closed my laptop and looked down at Max, already sleeping soundly. He was curled up next to me, snoring away. I stretched out under the covers, careful not to wake him.

That night I dreamed of ghosts and being trapped inside a house. I awoke with a start again. I looked at the clock, 3AM. What is it about 3AM that keeps waking me up? Once again I laid very quiet listening for any intruders, but heard nothing. Exhaustion took over and I eventually fell back to sleep. The next thing I knew, I felt a hot, smelly breath on my face. Max stood over me panting, waiting for me to wake up. As soon as I opened my eyes he jumped off the bed, ready for his morning exercise. I looked at the clock and couldn't believe it was 8:00AM. I never sleep past seven. I jumped out of bed. "Sorry, Max, I'm going to have to cut our walk short this morning." I threw on my shorts and t-shirt at the foot of the bed, slipped my feet into my tennis shoes by the door, quickly lacing them before racing outside with Max leading the way. I gave Max just enough time to do his business before returning home to get ready for work. I hurriedly showered and dressed in a flowery sun dress with sandals to ward off the heat before rushing to open the shop.

"You look like crap. Did you not sleep again last night?" Gloria asked as she entered the store.

"Thanks a lot. What a confidence booster you are. I did some research last night on the previous owners of my house. I had that on my mind when I fell asleep, giving me all kinds of weird dreams."

"What did you find out?"

"The previous owners' names were Herman and Dorothy Evanston. Did you know Dorothy was an artist?"

"Yes, I do remember something about that. The Woman's Club displayed one of her paintings during one of their craft fairs."

"There is an art dealer in New York that is listing some of her artwork for sale. If Dorothy Evanston had no family, I wonder how he acquired the pieces?"

"I assume she must have sold them before she passed away. Did you find anything in the house when you took ownership?"

"There was some dusty old furniture that was not worth anything that I hauled to the dump, but that was about it. It looked like everything of value had already been removed from the house before I arrived."

"You never know. Maybe they were stolen. The house was vacant for quite sometime before you bought it. I am sure there was plenty of opportunity for someone to go in and remove anything of value from the house without anyone knowing."

"I never thought about that. Maybe I should change the locks on the doors."

"It probably wouldn't be a bad idea. No telling who might have keys to the house."

I pondered the thought of someone coming into the house at night while I was sleeping.

9

The store had a steady stream of customers all morning and it was lunch time before I had time to take a break.

"Well, it's time for me to go. Hazel and I are going to lunch today. Will you be all right by yourself the rest of the day?" Gloria asked.

"Of course, go and have fun with Hazel."

The bell rang above the door as Gloria left. I felt strangely alone. I knelt down and patted Max, my forever companion, realizing how lucky I was to find him. I think he saved me from loneliness as much as I saved him. The mystery of Dorothy's artwork being for sale in New York intrigued me. I decided to call the art dealer to inquire about the paintings. I looked up the phone number online and called the gallery before I changed my mind. Strangely enough, as I listened for someone to answer the phone, I became anxious about what I might discover.

"Hello, I am calling about the Dorothy Evanston paintings you show for sale."

"Yes, she is a special artist and we are lucky to have a couple of her pieces."

"Do you mind telling me how they came to be in your possession?"

There was quiet on the other end of the line as I waited for a response. "I'm sorry, but I cannot divulge my source. Are you interested in purchasing one of Ms. Evanston's works?"

"No, not at this time." The line suddenly went dead before I could continue. That was quite strange. I looked at the receiver. "You didn't have to be so rude and hang up on me," I said out loud. I was startled when the phone started to ring. Maybe they called back to apologize, I thought.

"Hello."

"I was just calling to let you know that Gertrude told me about a large community garage sale on Saturday off East River Road. I bet you could find some new treasures for your store."

"Grandma, you wouldn't happen to want to go with me would you?" Grandma loved going to garage sales. The only problem, though, was she could never pass up a bargain. She was slowly filling my parent's house with the many deals she had purchased. My Dad warned me to stop taking her with me. There was no more room in their house or garage, for as my dad would say, "The junk," she brought home.

"You know I wouldn't pass up a chance to help you find merchandise for your store."

"Gloria can cover the store Saturday morning, so how about I pick you up at 7:30?" Dad is going to kill me, I thought to myself.

"Don't be late. You know all the good stuff gets sold early."

***

Saturday morning I pulled into my parents driveway at 7:30AM sharp and was greeted by my Dad as Grandma walked out of the house. Oh no, I hoped I wasn't going to get lectured on making sure Grandma doesn't buy anything. I stepped out of the car smiling and gave Dad a cheerful hug to try to put him in a good mood.

"How is your home remodeling going?" he asked.

"The house is coming along. I used five gallons of bleach to remove all the mold after having the plumbing fixed. Yeah! No more brown water is coming from the faucets. I'm currently working on the kitchen to freshen it up with some paint."

"You need to take a day off so I can take you fishing. The bass have really been biting lately."

"Gus told me how much fun you had last week fishing. I will definitely take you up on your offer soon. I could use a day on the river relaxing and soaking up some rays. I am so pale from working inside I look like one of the snow birds from up north," I laughed.

Grandma, now settled in my passenger seat, chimed in, "We better get going before all the deals are gone."

"Please don't let her bring home anymore junk," Dad whispered to me.

"I heard that. What you call junk could one day be worth a fortune," Grandma told him.

"I doubt that." My dad rolled his eyes and stepped away from the car as I backed down the driveway.

We arrived at the subdivision along with the swarm of other bargain hunters searching for the deal of a lifetime. We walked house to house as I sorted through the items for sale, looking for items I could sell and make a profit on. I found a vase and examined the bottom. It had been crafted in England. There were delicate flowers and birds hand painted on the side. I just hoped the owner didn't realize what she had, and offered her five dollars. I was pleased when she accepted my offer. I looked up to share my find with Grandma and realized she was nowhere in sight. This couldn't be good.

I worked my way back to my car and that's where I found Grandma trying to stuff three enormous, plastic, pink flamingos through the sun roof of my Ford Focus. "Grandma, what are you doing?"

"Aren't these beautiful? I only paid a dollar each for them. They will spiffy up the front yard of your parents house."

I am dead. My dad is never going to talk to me again, I thought to myself.

The morning was quickly heating up and after Grandma's purchase there was no more room in my small car. I drove Grandma home. When I arrived my Dad and his truck were nowhere in sight. I breathed a sigh of relief and quickly helped Grandma unload her bright pink flamingos.

"Let's put them over here underneath this palm tree. Now don't they look nice? They almost look lifelike."

I looked up to see my Dad's truck coming down the driveway. "I've got to run, Grandma. Thanks for going with me today." I rushed to escape in my car before Dad discovered Grandma's latest addition to his landscaping. I waved at Dad through my open window as I backed out of the driveway. As I pulled away I heard Dad yell, "What in the blazes are those things in my front yard?" I had a twinge of guilt as I drove away.

I swung by my house for a quick bite to eat and to pick up Max, then I raced to the store to share my latest treasures with Gloria. Since it was Saturday, the store was busy with customers all day. At first, I didn't notice when Sylvia walked in with her brother, Harper.

"Hey, Maggie, I was in town running errands with my brother and thought I would stop by to let you know my mother in-law loved her birthday present."

I looked up and couldn't take my eyes off Sylvia's brother. He was about six feet tall, with shaggy brown hair, deep blue eyes, and muscles bulging from underneath his t-shirt. I cleared my throat as I realized I was staring. "I'm sorry. What did you ask?"

"I didn't ask you anything. Are you feeling okay?"

I suddenly felt flush. "The summer heat must have gotten to me this morning at the garage sales," I quickly stated.

"I would like you to meet my brother, Harper."

"Nice to meet you. I heard you found a job locally, congratulations," I quickly blurted out.

"Yes, I start on Monday."

"Welcome back to town." I couldn't come up with anything more intelligent than that.

"Got to run," Sylvia spoke up. "Thanks again for the gift suggestion. See you on Friday evening to quilt."

I watched as Harper left. He definitely did not look anything like I had imagined. He must think I am an idiot.

"Well, well, isn't he good looking?" Gloria spoke up.

"Oh really, I didn't notice." I busied myself straightening a rack of vintage clothes, avoiding eye contact with Gloria.

"You can't fool me. I saw you staring at him. Why don't you suggest to Sylvia Friday night that you wouldn't mind if her brother asked you out?"

"Isn't it time for you to leave for the day? You must be tired after helping with customers all day."

"All right, I can take a hint. I'll see you on Tuesday. I bet Harper could lend you a hand fixing up your house. You should give him a call," Gloria added as she walked out the door.

"You never stop, do you?" I shouted to her.

# Three

Sunday after church I stopped by the home improvement store to pick up some more paint and a new light fixture for my bathroom. I was going through the many shades of rose colored paint, trying to decide which one would look best in my bathroom, when I turned to see Harper walking toward me. Like a shy schoolgirl I hid behind the paint display so I could spy on him. He seemed to be by himself as he turned down the electrical aisle. I casually pushed my shopping cart in that direction when all of a sudden Harper walked back out of the aisle and turned in my direction. I quickly turned down the plumbing aisle and pretended to look at toilets when I heard my name being called.

"Hey Maggie, I thought that was you. Sylvia told me you had recently bought one of the older homes in town. Are you replacing the toilet?"

"Yes," I lied to cover up the fact that I was spying on him. "It looks like you might be doing some work of your own." I pointed to the electrical outlet in his hand.

"Sylvia put me in the spare bedroom and the light switch is broken, so I thought I would fix it for her. Do you need help installing a new toilet? I know a little bit about plumbing."

"That's nice of you to offer, but I know you must be busy getting settled in and starting your new job."

"Nonsense. It shouldn't take long to install. Just point to the one you want and I can help load it in your car."

Since I really didn't need a new toilet I pointed to the cheapest model. Harper placed it on my cart along with the seal and other items I would need. As I checked out I prayed I had enough balance left on my credit card to cover the expense. It

15

came to just under two hundred dollars, which I really couldn't afford.

Harper followed me home and helped unload my car. Max greeted us at the door and then proceeded to smell Harper's legs and feet to make sure our guest was safe.

"Who do we have here?" Harper asked.

"This is Max, my very friendly golden retriever."

"Aren't you a big boy?" Harper said as he rubbed Max's ears which was all Max needed to totally accepted his new friend.

"Would you like some lunch before we get started?" I asked.

"No, I'm good. I had a late breakfast. Just show me where you want it installed."

My bedroom and bathroom were a total disaster area with clothes and towels laying all over the floor. I hadn't had time to pick up and do laundry yet this week. I didn't want Harper thinking I lived like a pig, so I steered him away from my room. "The guest bathroom is this way."

"I like your house. It has many interesting architectural characteristics. I actually studied a semester of architecture before I changed my degree. I always loved the mystique of old homes."

"I guess you could call bad plumbing, warped floors and a leaky roof mystical," I laughed. "Here is the bathroom."

"The toilet looks practically new. Are you sure you want to replace it?"

Knowing I had just replaced it a few weeks ago I played dumb and said, "It hasn't been flushing right."

"All you may need is a new toilet fill valve. Did you check that?"

"No, what is that?" I asked, like a ditzy blond. This is my way out of spending two hundred dollars I didn't have, I thought to myself.

"I'll take a look." He lifted the lid off the toilet and pushed the handle to flush it. "It appears to be working fine now. Maybe it's just sticking occasionally."

A loud crash came from the hall and I jumped. I could only imagine what had broken now. I hurried out of the bathroom and ran down the hall. Two books were lying on the floor again. "I've been having trouble with these books falling off the shelf of this bookcase. Maybe the floor is warped," I tried to rationalize. "Gloria thinks I have ghost," I joked.

Harper helped me pick up the books. "It looks like you're a history buff."

Max started to whine and leaned against my leg for protection. "What is it boy?" I asked as I rubbed his head to calm him down.

"Most dogs have a sixth sense about things we cannot detect," Harper commented.

"Not this dog. He is just chicken and doesn't like loud noises. I'm sorry to waste your time today. It looks like I might not need a new toilet after all."

"No problem. Give me a call if your toilet starts acting up again and I'll come over and try to fix it for you."

Harper left and the house seemed eerily quiet. I went into the kitchen and helped myself to a large bowl of chocolate ice cream. I had blown almost the entire day and had gotten nothing accomplished around the house. I was still unsettled about the books falling again and decided to go online to examine the artwork that Dorothy had painted more closely. I opened the gallery website and strangely the pieces were no longer displayed. Surely the gallery couldn't have sold them all in such a short time. Additional searches proved fruitless.

On the way to bed I stopped in the hall and looked at the bookcase. I pushed on several books to make sure they were securely in place. I still couldn't explain why the books kept finding themselves on the floor. I removed one of the books that had previously fallen and glanced at the cover. It was on the many different Indians tribes that had lived in Florida. I leafed through the pages, stopping to examine a picture of an Indian mound located just outside Palatka. I found the fact amazing that eight hundred years ago Indians lived in the Florida heat without air conditioning and made these enormous mounds with their bare hands and no machinery. They walked miles to transport the dirt and shells. All this effort just to bury their dead and possessions. The perils they must have lived through. They had to have been plagued with disease from the swarms of mosquitos, not to mention the numerous venomous snakes that must have populated the area during that time. It gave me the chills thinking about the hardships they must have endured. Dorothy's paintings, the books falling, Indian mounds...none of this made any sense. Was there somehow a connection between them? My brain was too tired to think any more and I went to bed.

I spent another restless night tossing and turning in bed. I was jarred awake by another loud noise. This time I was sure someone was in the house as Max started to growl. A low, deep noise rose from his throat as he stared at the door. I quietly pulled my revolver from the night stand and pointed it at the door, waiting for whoever might walk through it. I should have changed the locks after Gloria had told me that anyone could have a key to the house, I thought to myself. Then I heard the back door slam and a car drive away. Gun still in hand and Max by my side, I turned on every light in the house making sure I was alone. I checked the back door and the lock had been broken. I looked around the house to see if anything was missing. I didn't have a lot and everything seemed to be in place. Maybe the sound of Max growling scared them away before they could steal anything. Wide awake now and not sure what I should do, I called Dad.

Dad called his friend, the police chief, and they were both at my house within ten minutes. I explained what little I knew. They both felt it was probably someone looking for some quick cash who got scared off. The police chief indicated that he would have an officer check for prints in the morning, but doubted they would find any.

"I would feel better if you came home with me until the lock can be replaced tomorrow. You can sleep in your old room."

"I guess you're right. I probably wouldn't be able to sleep anymore here tonight anyway," I said as I threw a few things in a duffel bag and loaded Max into my car.

My old room was just as I left it, with stuffed animals on the bed, high school year books on the bookshelf, and blue ribbons from my days on the swim team. Exhausted, I crawled into bed, pushing the stuffed animals aside. Surprisingly, Max and I fell fast asleep with the comfort of knowing I was safe in my old bed. Many nights of little sleep had caught up with me.

I awoke to the sound of Grandma talking loudly in the kitchen about the coffee being too strong. Grandma never liked it when Dad made the coffee. She always accused him of making bad coffee on purpose so she wouldn't drink any.

I announced my presence, "Dad, I could use a cup of your strong brew."

"What are you doing here? Did the ghost drive you from your place? Gertrude is always telling me about how those old homes are haunted."

"No, Grandma there are no ghosts in my house. Just someone trying to break in."

"It was probably one of those druggies. We are not safe anywhere any more. You need to get you a big guard dog. That will scare them away."

"Grandma, I have Max and don't need another dog. It was probably someone who thought the house was still vacant." I tried to make light of the situation, but was not sure I convinced myself that it was nothing.

"I will pick you up some new locks and dead bolts for the doors and install them this morning," Dad spoke up.

"Thanks Dad, I appreciate that."

"Your mother has been up worrying about you all night and wants you to sell the house," Dad whispered to me as Mom's concerned tired face appeared in the door.

"Good morning, Mom. Sorry to wake you last night. Dad is going to fix my locks today so you don't have to worry."

19

"I knew it was not a good idea for a young girl like you to get her own place."

"Mom, I am twenty-three years old and run my own business. I am not a little girl. I will be fine."

"You need to find a husband so you're not alone in that house by yourself every night."

Oh Lord, here it comes, I think to myself. "I'm not alone. I have Max there to protect me."

"Are you dating anyone? Mrs. Utinsky's nephew is staying with her for the summer. He is working on his masters degree. Why don't I invite him over for supper one night so you can meet him?"

"Mom, I don't need your help in finding a husband for me."

"When is the last time you went out on a date?"

"I've been a bit busy with my business and new house to have time to date. Dad, we better get to the hardware store so we can get those locks fixed."

Dad understood instantly. "You're right, we better get going." He grabbed his truck keys and headed for the door.

"You didn't even eat any breakfast," Mom yelled as I made my escape.

"I'm good." I raised my cup of coffee in the air. "I will grab a bite to eat later," I yelled back as Dad backed out of the driveway.

"Thanks for saving me back there. I just couldn't take Mom badgering me this morning about getting married."

"She is only worried about you."

"I know, but I don't think she realizes I am a grown woman and don't need a guy to take care of me. I can take care of myself. Oh, that reminds me. Can you stop by my house on the way to the store? I need to return the toilet I bought yesterday."

"I thought you just replaced the toilet a few weeks ago."

"I did. It's a long story. Did you go fishing last night?" I quickly changed the subject.

"The fish have really been biting at the croaker hole. Maybe Wednesday evening after work I can take you fishing. We can both relax while we wait for the big ones to take our bait."

"That sounds just like what I need." I don't truly know if I enjoy the fishing as much as just being out on the river enjoying the view, relaxing, and spending time with Dad. When I was growing up that was the one time I had Dad all to myself. Mom was never much for fishing, so this was something I could do alone with him. I can still remember catching my first fish when I was very young. Dad was more excited about the fact that I hooked a fish than me. It was as if me catching a fish was somehow a reflection of his parenting skills. The art of fishing can be a soul searching activity. Sitting on the river sometimes for hours without even a bite gives you much time to reflect and be thankful for what you have. Watching the osprey and eagles fish, the occasional manatee passing by or otter playing along the shoreline makes you realize what life is truly all about. The patience Dad taught me while fishing will carry me throughout my life.

Dad pulled into the hardware store parking lot and I retrieved a shopping cart for Dad to place the toilet on. I returned the toilet while Dad found me new locks. I now had enough money to buy the gallon of paint I needed for the bathroom, that I had intended to buy the last time I was here when Harper surprised me.

While Dad changed the locks, I prepared the bathroom for painting by cleaning the walls and applying masking tape around the window. It was not long before Dad yelled, "All done with the locks. I'm going to head out unless you need anything else."

I brushed myself off and walked into the kitchen. Dad handed me my new keys. I tried them in the new dead bolt and lock. "They worked great, turning easily. I will sleep so much better tonight knowing the doors are secure. I will see you after work on Wednesday to go fishing. Thanks Dad!"

"Lock the doors after I leave. Call me tonight if you hear any more strange noises."

Dad left and the house seemed eerily quiet. Paranoia was starting to get the best of me. I felt like someone was watching me. I told myself I was just being silly. Then the phone rang and I about jumped out of my skin.

I quickly grabbed the receiver, "Hello."

"Hi, it's Harper. I was just checking to see if you were having any more trouble with your toilet?"

"No, it seems to be working fine now. Whatever you did seemed to have fixed it." Maggie felt guilty for lying to him.

"Would you like to go out for dinner one night this week?"

"That would be nice. My shop closes at six so I could be ready by seven."

"How does Wednesday sound?"

I cringed. "I am supposed to go fishing with my Dad that night. Can we make it Thursday instead?"

"Sure, no problem. I will see you Thursday at seven."

An overwhelming sense of happiness came over me. My mind was suddenly full of what I should wear. My nails were a mess. I needed a manicure. I tried to refocus on painting the bathroom, with little luck. I had a date to prepare for.

# Four

The next few nights were uneventful with no strange noises during the night. I was finally able to sleep undisturbed, well that is until Max woke me up, eager to start the day. Wednesday after work I met Dad to go fishing. Unfortunately, the fish weren't biting, but the bugs sure were. Between the mosquitos and gnats, all I did was swat myself all night long. I had applied bug repellent on my arms and legs, but it didn't seem to help much. I glanced at Dad, sitting quietly at the other end of the boat, just calmly fishing. He was either ignoring the bugs or they weren't biting him. I was relieved when Dad said, "Well, I guess the fish aren't hungry. We might as well call it a night and go home."

The boat motor turned over and within seconds the breeze as we raced through the water provided me relief from the bugs. Ten minutes later we were back at the boat ramp, loaded the boat back on the trailer and headed home.

Once home I took off my fishing clothes and jumped into the shower to wash the stench of bug spray and smashed bugs off of me. I toweled off and wiped the steam from the mirror. I cringed when I saw my face. It was covered in red blotches where I had been bitten by mosquitos. I looked like I had chicken pox. In less than twenty-four hours Harper would be picking me up for our date. I couldn't let him see me like this. I lathered myself in cortisone cream hoping that would help. I crawled into bed but the itching was unbearable. I scratched my arms, face, and legs until I finally fell asleep.

The next morning Gloria greeted me at the store. "What the devil happened to you? It looks like you walked into a bee hive."

"I went fishing with Dad last night and the bug repellent didn't work." My face was all swollen from scratching all night long.

"Have you tried vinegar? Sometimes that will relieve the itching."

"No, at this point I will try anything. Can you watch the shop while I run to the store to buy some?"

"I'm sure I can manage without you for a little while," Gloria said sarcastically.

I returned a little while later with cotton balls and vinegar. I dabbed some on my arms and face. Gloria crinkled her nose up at me. "I smell bad, don't I?"

"No, it just reminds me of the days when I used to make pickles with my Mom. I never wanted to see another cucumber after that."

"Even though I smell atrocious the coolness of the vinegar does seem to help the itching."

The day dragged on and finally six o'clock came so I could close the store.

"You're in a hurry tonight. Do you have a hot date?" Gloria asked.

I didn't want Gloria to know I was going out with Harper or the whole town would know by morning. "No, I just want to get home so I can relax and take a long, soothing bath," I lied.

I rushed into the house and Max ran to his food dish. I fed him and had thirty minutes to shower and change before Harper arrived. I gently washed trying to remove the smell of vinegar without causing the itching to return. I covered myself in cologne and put concealer all over my face to hide my blotches. The doorbell rang just as I was slipping my feet into sandals to go with my lightweight flowery sun dress. I wore my long dirty blond hair down over my shoulders to cover the bug bites on my neck. I took a deep breath and slowly exhaled as I opened the door.

"You look nice. Are you ready to go?"

"Thanks, let me just grab my keys." Max ran to greet Harper as I searched for where I had left my keys. After searching just about everywhere I discovered I had thrown them on my bed. I returned to find Harper playing with Max in the living room. I smiled at the sight.

"Found them!" I announced as I held my keys in the air.

Harper patted Max on the head. "Got to go, boy. We will have to finish this game later."

"Stay out of trouble while I'm gone," I instructed Max as if he could understand.

The evening was going well. I concentrated on not itching my bug bites while I listened to Harper tell me about himself.

"You seem quiet tonight. Is everything okay?" he asked.

Oh Lord, do I tell Harper the truth and come clean about being eaten alive by bugs? I bit my bottom lip and explained the adventure with my Dad the previous night. After I finished telling him about covering myself in vinegar to stop the itching he broke out into laughter.

"Is that what I smell? I've been trying to figure it out all night long."

I blushed from embarrassment. "I guess I haven't been very good company tonight."

"You should have told me sooner. I could have rescheduled."

I was pleased that Harper was so understanding. The waiter brought the check and Harper drove me home.

To ease my pain Harper told me a story of when he was a little boy he dove into some bushes to catch a football. Unbeknown to him, there was poison ivy growing all over the bushes he dove into.

I was still laughing when Harper pulled into my driveway, as he described how he itched in places he had never itched before. "It's still early. Would you like to come in and watch TV for a while?"

"Do you feel up to it?"

"If you can stand the smell. I'm fine."

Max greeted us at the door and jumped on Harper. "Hey, Max!" Harper cheerfully said as he rubbed Max's ears.

"Max get down. You know better than to jump on people."

"No problem, I love dogs. I had a dog growing up when I was a kid."

"Oh, what type of dog did you have?"

"It was part lab and about ten other breeds. He showed up in our yard one day half starved, so I sneake him some food without my parents knowing. After dark I let him into my bedroom through the window. The next morning when my Mom came to wake me up for school she found the filthy dog in bed with me. To say she was a little angry was an understatement. But after a while I was able to wear her down. She agreed to let me keep the dog if I made sure it was bathed, fed, and walked each day."

"I bet he was your best friend after that."

"Yes, he patiently waited for me to return each day at the school bus stop. Talk about unconditional love. It broke my heart the day I had to put him down. His hips gave out and he could no longer walk."

"That's so sad. I know what you mean. I don't know what I would do without Max. He has been my constant companion now for four years." Max lifted his head as he heard his name being mentioned. I rubbed behind his ears to let him know how much I loved him.

I turned on the television and scrolled through the guide. "The Big Bang Theory is on. Do you want to watch that?"

"Yes, that's one of my favorite shows."

I felt so relaxed around Harper. We laughed together at the jokes as we watched the show. All of a sudden I heard a loud thump. I hoped the intruder hadn't returned, I thought to myself. "Did you hear that noise?"

"It sounded like it came from above our heads."

We both walked outside and looked up at the roof. "I don't see anything," Harper said.

"It must have been squirrels jumping from the trees and running across the roof," I tried to rationalize.

We retreated back inside to finish watching the show. A few minutes later we heard a louder bang.

"Do you have an attic?" Harper asked.

"I do, but I've never ventured up there. I figured it was probably better not knowing what was up there. I am not thrilled with spiders and bugs."

"Get me a flashlight and I'll check to see if I can find the source of the noise."

I rummaged through the kitchen junk drawer. "Here you go." I handed Harper a flashlight.

"The attic stairs are at the end of the hallway." I showed Harper the way.

Harper pulled on the cord hanging from the ceiling. The stairs unfolded in front of him. He stepped on the first step to make sure they were secure and safe. He shined the flashlight toward the opening.

"Be careful, there is probably all kinds of poisonous spiders up there," I cautioned him.

Harper disappeared into the dark space as I waited for him to return. "Do you see anything?" I yelled up. There was no response. Visions of ghosts and rats crossed my mind. I hesitated, trying to decide if I should venture up the stairs to check on him. Worried something had happened to Harper, I cautiously climbed the ladder. Just as I was about to reach the top of the opening Harper suddenly appeared. I shrieked, "You scared the living daylights out of me1 Why didn't you answer when I called?"

"I'm sorry. I didn't hear you. Come here, you have got to see this."

Harper offered me his hand as I stepped into the dark attic.

"This way." He shined the light toward the window at the far end of the attic. There was an easel standing by the window with

27

containers of paint and art supplies laying on the floor. There was an unfinished painting on the easel.

"This must have belonged to Dorothy." I explained to Harper about finding Dorothy's paintings online at an art gallery in New York and how after I contacted the dealer the paintings were removed from the web site. "Do you think someone stole those paintings from her after she died?"

"There is no telling. From the way you described Dorothy, she sounded like a recluse. That does not sound like the type of person who would sell art work in New York. She lived here most of her life and rarely left her house. Do you really think she would let an art dealer in New York sell her paintings?"

"You're right, something definitely does not add up. This painting looks as if it's almost complete. She must have been working on it just before she died."

I studied the painting of large oak trees with the Spanish moss blowing in the wind. In the background was the St Johns River with a sailboat floating by. The brightly colored sails billowed in the breeze. It looked to be a typical day along the river. I reached to touch the painting to feel if the paint was still wet. It looked so real. "I wish I had met Dorothy. She was such a talented artist."

"Well, I am afraid I didn't find the source of your noise. You were probably right, it must have been squirrels scurrying along the roof en route to another tree."

"Thanks for checking. I feel better knowing there is nothing hiding in my attic. It's getting late and I know you have to be at work early tomorrow. I better let you go."

We climbed back down the ladder and Harper closed the attic door for me. I sneezed as I brushed the dust and cobwebs from my hair.

Harper smiled as he watched me. His deep blue eyes bored into my soul, leaving me feeling naked. I regained my composure and walked him to the door.

Harper leaned down and kissed me gently on the lips. "I hear the dirt track is open for the summer. Would you like to go with me to the races Saturday night?"

"That sounds like fun. I haven't been in ages. Thanks for dinner tonight and I am sorry I was not better company."

"The vinegar smell grew on me as the evening went on," he laughed. "How about I pick you up at seven on Saturday?"

"Can't wait." I smiled. I closed the door and rolled my eyes. I couldn't come up with a better response than that to end the evening? Harper must think I am an idiot. He was just as nice as he looked, I smiled to myself. I went to bed feeling elated. After little sleep the night before from itching I drifted off to sleep quickly.

It seemed like I had slept for just a very short time when I awoke to a loud noise. Not again. I looked at the clock, 3AM. What is it about 3AM? I quietly climbed out of bed and grabbed my revolver from the night stand. "Thank you Dad for teaching me how to shoot and spending all those days at the gun range with me," I whispered to myself. I opened my bedroom door and Max suddenly appeared by my side. I am not sure if he was protecting me or I him. I peered down the hall. The moon was full tonight, illuminating my path. I approached the bookcase and saw the same two books were on the floor again. I reached down to pick them up when I heard a shuffling noise coming from the attic. The attic stairs were up, so no one could be up there, I rationalized. There was no way I was going to go up in the attic in the middle of the night to face whatever varmint may be running around. I decided to wait until morning to venture any further. I picked the two books up off the floor, once again, and brought them back to bed with me. Knowing I wouldn't be getting anymore sleep tonight, I turned on my lamp and glanced through the books on Florida's history. Strangely, a page on the Spanish occupation of Florida had been folded over. I read how Spain had occupied Florida in the early 1800s staying in the same area as the Seminole Indians before England took over. The St. Johns River provided the means to travel to the coast. This area was very fertile and

29

produced many foods needed for the settlers to survive. It was an ideal location to live. The Seminole Indians were driven from the area by the British during the Seminole War of 1833. It's so sad that our ancestors couldn't learn to live peacefully with the Indians. We never seem to learn from our past. It's easier to make war than to live in peace.

I drifted off to sleep with thought of Indians living peacefully along the river. I awoke to the sunshine streaming through my window. The book still laid open on my bed to the section on the Spanish occupation of Florida. I didn't have time to dwell on what it may all mean, and hurried to take Max for a walk.

# Five

Gloria happily greeted me as always Friday morning. "Are you feeling better today?"

"Much. I hardly notice the itching this morning."

"See, using the vinegar helped."

"How was your date with Harper?"

"How did you know I had a date with him?"

"I ran into Sylvia at the grocery store last night. You know you can't hide anything from me," Gloria laughed.

"We had a very nice time. Oh, I discovered a painting of Dorothy's in the attic last night. I heard a noise and Harper helped me investigate."

"Well, wasn't that nice of him."

"Stop with the insinuations. We just watched TV. Do you think someone could have broken into Dorothy's house after she died and stole her paintings?"

"That's very possible. With all the snow birds in this area, who leave their homes unattended for months, I am sure this area is more prone to burglaries."

"Maybe whoever broke in before is the one who broke my lock Sunday night."

"Have you heard anything from the police?"

"No, the person probably didn't leave any prints. I just wonder what he was looking for since nothing appeared to be missing."

The bell on the door rang and I looked up to see Melanie, a friend of Gloria's walk in. She often stopped by to catch up on the latest gossip. "Did you hear the Galveston place was broken into last night?"

"Maggie, isn't that house just down the road from you? Maybe it's the same person that broke into your house."

"Do you know if anything was taken?"

"The family cat jumped on the burglar and scared him before he could steal anything."

"I bet that surprised him. I've heard of using a guard dog but never a guard cat!" Gloria laughed.

"Was anyone other than the cat home," I asked.

"The Galveston's had returned early from a summer vacation. Mr. Galveston fell ill so they ended their trip early. They were not supposed to have been back until Sunday."

Gloria chimed in, "You know what you need is a neighborhood watch. We started one in my neighborhood last year. We put up signs to warn burglars that we are watching and we take turns driving around the neighborhood each month and report any suspicious activity to the police."

"Have you caught any burglars?"

"No, but I saw Mr. Collins visiting Mrs. Thacker late one night, which I thought was strange."

"They are both in their eighties so not much could be going on," Melanie giggled. "I've got to run. Albert should be finished with his golf game soon and will want something to eat as soon as he arrives home."

"Now where were we? Oh yes, you were telling me about your date with Harper."

"There is nothing more to tell. I wish I could find out how the art dealer in New York came to be in possession of Dorothy's paintings. I've got a feeling it was not by legal means."

"I've an idea. Why don't I give them a call pretending to be an art enthusiast and see what I can find out?"

"That would be great! They may recognize my voice if I call again. Here is their phone number."

Gloria picked up the phone on the counter, punched in the phone number and waited for someone to answer as I paced anxiously. "Hello, friend of mine from Long Island recently viewed a painting in your studio from an artist name Dorothy Evanston. She told me it would look perfect in my great room. Do you by any chance still have the painting?"

I waited impatiently while Gloria listened to the response on the other end of the phone.

"You have three paintings by her and need to know which one I am interested in." Gloria looked at me for assistance.

"The painting of the lighthouse," I whispered.

Gloria repeated what I said over the phone.

"Tell him you want to validate the authenticity before you purchase the painting," I whispered.

"Oh, I am so glad you haven't sold it. Can you provide me the name of the person you procured the painting from so I can verify the authenticity?"

"Thank you so much for your help." Continuing on with her act she added, "I will make arrangements to buy the painting and be in touch." Gloria hung up the phone.

I was not able to contain myself any longer and yelled, "What did he say?"

"Walter Henderson, who was a friend of the family, supposedly contacted the art dealer for Dorothy to sell her paintings."

"Yes1" I jumped with excitement. "You were great! Do you know a Walter Henderson?"

"No, but why don't we look up the name in the white pages and see if he lives in Putnam County."

Even though Putnam County is large it's mostly rural with many farms. The phone list is short compared to most counties. Gloria and I ran our fingers down the directory looking through the H's for Henderson. "There he is," I yelled. "Walter Henderson lives on Avocado Way in Pomona Park. Do you think we should give him a call?"

"I'm not sure. What do we say? Do we ask him how he knew Dorothy and how he came to be in possession of her paintings? If he stole the paintings then he may run before we can get any answers. Let's see what we can find out about him first before we contact him," Gloria rationalized.

Our search would have to wait. The bell above the door sounded as a customer entered.

After the last patron for the day left, I breathed a sigh of relief. "The girls from the quilting club will be here any minute. I better hurry to close up and set everything out for them," I told Gloria.

I created the quilting club to help bring business to the store but it ended up being more of a girls night out for some of the wives in the community. A couple of bottles of wine are consumed while the women talk about their week and enjoy each other's company. Tonight Sylvia, Audrey, Valerie, Cynthia, and Joanne showed up to enjoy the evening with me and Gloria. Some nights between the talking, drinking, and laughing not a lot of quilting gets done.

Gloria shared the mystery of Dorothy's paintings while the women ate Sylvia's luscious brownies and drank themselves silly with wine. "Do you know a Walter Henderson who lives in Pomona Park?" Gloria asked the group.

No one had heard of him which was strange. There is one thing I've learned about these women; they know just about everyone in town and no matter what happens they will know before morning. Their phone lines are faster than any newspaper publication when it came to hearing about the latest news.

Audrey, who is in her thirties, a mother of two boys, ages eight and ten, and works in the tax collectors office spoke up. "I can help discover who Walter Henderson is. I can tell you his income, where he works, what kind of car he drives and if he has ever been arrested."

"That would be wonderful, but I wouldn't want you to get into any trouble at work," I said with a concerned look on my face.

"It's part of my job to keep the files on the citizens of Putnam County current so it shouldn't raise any flags. I will let you know what I find on Monday."

With that being settled Gloria and Sylvia brought the women up to date on my date with Harper.

"Tell us all about it," Valerie begged. Valerie married her high school sweetheart as soon as she turned eighteen, has been married fifteen years and has three kids. She is always trying to fix me up and get me married off to someone. She is a full time housewife that enjoys being a mother and loving wife. She prays I will find the love of my life so I can experience that same happiness one day.

"There is nothing to tell. Harper took me out to eat and then we watched TV at my house."

"What about hearing the noises and sneaking around the attic together? You forgot to tell them about that," Gloria chimed in.

"I've been hearing a lot of strange noises since I moved into my house. Last night it sounded like someone or something was in the attic. I hadn't ventured up there since I bought the house a month ago so Harper volunteered to check it out for me."

"Wasn't that brave of him?" Valerie joked.

I ignored Valerie's comment and continued. "I thought there might be a raccoon or squirrel up there. What Harper found, though, was an unfinished painting and art supplies. Dorothy must have used the space to paint. The unfinished painting is of the river as seen outside the attic window. The painting kind of makes me feel sad for Dorothy. I can imagine her sitting alone in the dark musty attic for hours while she painted. She created such beautiful works of art, depicting the world around her, but rarely left the house to experience life."

"I would go nuts if I stayed in my house all day long," Valerie said. "That's so strange. What do you think scared Dorothy so much that she never left her house?"

"Maybe Mr. Evanston was very controlling and didn't want her leaving the house," Gloria added.

"Maybe she was just an introvert, like me, who was comfortable by herself and found it difficult to socialize with others," Cynthia quietly said as she looked down and continued to sew her quilt.

"Cynthia, I never considered you an introvert. I always thought of you as polite, a good listener and someone you could count on if needed," I said.

Cynthia blushed. "I don't think Dorothy was unhappy at all. She just found a way to express herself through her paintings rather than going out in public."

"Joanne, how are things going at the women's shelter?" I asked. Joanne was in a very abusive relationship with her husband for years. When she tried to leave him he almost killed her. Since her husband controlled all the finances, she had no money and no one she could ask for help to stay with. If it was not for a kind grandmotherly type woman seeing her bruises one day and offering her assistance, she might have ended up dead. She was so grateful to the woman for helping her get her life back that she wanted to do the same thing for other women needing to get-a-way from an abusive relationship. After working in a department store and quickly being promoted to manager she saved enough money to open a house where women could stay until they could get their lives back on track.

"Very good. Two of my residents moved out this week after finding jobs and an apartment they could afford."

The evening ended with everyone a little tipsy from the wine, but it was nice to be able to spend time together with friends. I arrived home, exhausted once again. After feeding Max I collapsed in bed and fell fast asleep. I awoke with a start from a deep sleep, feeling uneasy. Foggy from being woken up suddenly, I wondered if I had truly heard a noise or did I dream it. I looked at the clock, 3AM. Not again. What is it about 3AM that this house won't let me sleep? I wondered. I lay quietly and heard the wind rustling the leaves of the large live oak tree outside my window, then I heard a faint noise in the attic. I can't go on like this, never getting a full night's sleep. Frustrated, I grabbed the flashlight and my revolver out of the night stand and slipped out of bed. I walked down the hall toward the attic door. I shined the flashlight at the closed attic door and listened. I heard the sound of soft footsteps again from above my head. I gathered up my courage and pulled down the attic steps. I quietly walked up the stairs and stopped when I reached the top, peeking my head just through the opening. The almost full moon shined through the attic window illuminating the space. I didn't need the flashlight to see. I looked toward the end of the attic where the easel with Dorothy's unfinished painting stood. A wispy figure of a woman sat in front of the easel. I stared in disbelief, thinking that I must be dreaming. I dared not move or I might wake up and the figure would disappear. The figure turned her head and looked at me. I was mesmerized by her sky blue eyes staring into my soul as if trying to communicate with me. Amazingly enough I was not scared, but I stayed calm as I studied the ghost of who must have been Dorothy. Dorothy turned back to her unfinished painting and continued to paint. She looked at me again over her shoulder, then at the painting. Dorothy lifted her wispy hand and pointed at her painting as if trying to show me something. I eased into the attic, trying to see what she was pointing at when a cloud suddenly drifted in front of the moon and I was thrown into darkness. I quickly reached for the flashlight in my hand and turned it on. I pointed the light toward where Dorothy's ghost was last seen. She was gone. I walked toward the easel and looked at the unfinished painting. The painting captured the scene outside the window looking out toward the river. She had captured the old stone walkway and trees that lined the street. What was she pointing at? The stone walk way? I looked out the attic window, trying to imagine what it must have been like for Dorothy all alone after her husband died. The dim glow from the street light at the corner shed little light on the front yard. The neighborhood looked peaceful and quiet for this time of night. Still perplexed with what I had seen I carefully climbed down the attic stairs and found Max waiting for me at the bottom, whining. "What is it boy? Did something scare you?" I turned on the hall light and saw the

Palatka history book had fallen off the shelf again onto the floor. The page showing when Spain occupied the state lay open on the floor. I picked up the book and read the story on how the Spaniards had killed the Indians then settled in the area along the river until England invaded. "Dorothy, what are you trying to tell me?" I spoke out load in case she could hear me.

I couldn't sleep the rest of the night and laid awake thinking about Dorothy and her paintings. As the sun came up, I dragged myself out of bed, at the delight of Max. I put Max's leash on and we went for our morning walk along the river, enjoying the cool morning breeze. I couldn't get Dorothy off my mind. I ran into my neighbor and politely said, "Good morning," as Max fertilized the grass around a tree. "Mrs. Avery, by any chance did you know the Evanston's that lived in my house?" I asked before she could get-a-way.

"Yes, I did. They were very good neighbors, always keeping their yard and house looking very nice. That's until Mr. Evanston passed away. It was just too much for Dorothy to keep up. I stopped by several times to check in on her. She was always very nice, inviting me in for tea. The inside of her house was lovely. She had antique furniture throughout the house and displayed her beautiful paintings in several of the rooms. She was so talented."

"What happened to her artwork after she passed away?" I played dumb to see what information she knew.

"I don't know. I just assumed whatever family she had left received them. Now that you mention it though, I don't remember seeing any pictures of family in the house and Dorothy never talked about having a brother or sister."

Max was done with his business and pulled on his leash to remind me it was time to continue our walk. "Have a nice day Mrs. Avery," I yelled as I was pulled along by Max.

Saturday was my busy day at the store and I didn't get a chance to tell Gloria about seeing Dorothy's ghost. I started to wonder whether I had imagined the whole thing due to exhaustion.

I raced home from worked and quickly changed into capris, a cool strapless top and sandals just in time for Harper to arrive for our date. He took me to the dirt race track in Satsuma where we watched as the funny cars skidded around the course roaring by after each lap. We pigged out on hot dogs and soda while we cheered along with the crowd rooting for the underdog to come from behind and win the race. I felt so comfortable around Harper. The uneasiness I had felt during our first date was gone and we joked and laughed all night long. Harper took me home after the race and we continued talking and laughing about the condition of some of the cars racing as pieces fell off after each lap. We wondered if they would make it to the finish line before breaking down. By the end of the night the number of cars still running and in one piece was reduced by a few. It was near eleven o'clock when we arrived at my house. I didn't want the evening to end. Harper leaned over and gave me a kiss. His lips touched mine tenderly. "Would you like to come in for a while? I promise I won't make you go back up in the attic to look for critters," I laughed.

"You never know what could be lurking inside. I better make sure it's safe," Harper joked.

I opened the door and looked around half expecting to see Dorothy's ghost waiting for me. The house was quiet. I microwaved some popcorn and cuddled up next to Harper while we watched a movie.

"You seem distracted since we got home. Is something wrong?"

"I'm sorry. Something weird happened last night and I can't get it out of my mind."

"What happened?"

"You're probably going to think I am crazy, but here goes. I saw Dorothy's ghost last night in the attic and I think she is trying to tell me something."

"What do you think she is trying to tell you?"

"I'm not sure. She kept pointing to her unfinished painting upstairs."

"I always love a good mystery. Let's go back up in the attic and take another look at the painting."

"You believe me!" I said in amazement.

"Of course, why wouldn't I? There are all kinds of strange things that cannot be explained in this world. What happens after we die is just one of them. There are several accounts of ghosts in the old graveyards in the area, so why would I not believe you saw one last night?"

I leaned over and gave Harper a kiss.

"I will have to agree with you more often if that means I will get a kiss," Harper teased.

We climbed back up into the attic and I shined the flashlight on the unfinished painting on the easel. "What do you think she was trying to tell me?"

Harper looked at the painting of the wind swept oak trees and yard below. "I think we need more info. What do you know about the Evanstons?"

"Well, they moved here in the early 50's not long after they were married. Herman worked at the local pulp and paper processing plant helping to clear the timber used to make the products at the mill. Dorothy and Herman never had any children. Herman had a heart attack and passed away. Dorothy was found dead in the house about six months later. Oh, and for some reason a book on Palatka history with the page on the Spanish settlement keeps falling open on the floor."

"Definitely strange. You're right, you certainly have a mystery on your hand and I've no idea what it all means."

"Maybe Walter Henderson can help."

"Who is Walter Henderson?"

"Oh, I forgot to tell you. Gloria and I found out that he is the person who sold Dorothy's paintings to the art gallery in New York. Audrey is supposed to call me on Monday with information on him and what his relationship was with the Evanstons."

"Don't do anything rash. You may be stirring up something that may be better off left undisturbed." Harper leaned down and kissed me on the forehead.

"Well, it's getting late and I don't think we can solve your mystery tonight."

"How about you come over after work on Monday around seven? I can fix us something to eat and let you know what Audrey discovered on Walter Henderson."

"Sounds good." Harper stopped at the door, leaned down and gently kissed me again before leaving for the night. He tasted of salt left over from the popcorn we had eaten. My heart ached as I watched him leave. I knew I was in trouble. I was falling in love.

# Six

I awoke Sunday morning to the phone ringing. With my eyes still closed I groped for the receiver and answered it. "Hello," I mumbled.

"Maggie, did I wake you?"

I looked at the clock. Seven o'clock. "Mom, is something wrong? Why are you calling me so early?"

"I heard you had a date last night. Mrs. Parker from down the street called and told me she saw you at the races with a good looking boy. Who are you seeing and why didn't you tell me you had a boyfriend?"

"Mom, we are just friends."

"You should bring him to supper with you tonight so your father and I can meet him."

"I am not bringing him to supper, Mom. Goodbye, I am going to finish sleeping now." I hung up, knowing I would never get back to sleep. Max laid his large head across my chest, looking pitiful. His sad eyes pleaded with me to get up and take him for a walk. "All right, I give up of ever getting another good night's rest. Between you and Dorothy's ghost it's hopeless." Max jumped off the bed and ran toward the door, barking excessively. I know he was telling me to hurry up in dog talk.

Bass boats lined the boat ramp this morning as eager fishermen launched their boats in hopes of catching the big one. The St. Johns River is known for its fantastic fishing. There are several springs and deep holes where the fish love to hide in the summer time. Fishermen from all over the country come to Palatka to compete in the fishing tournaments held here. Birds lined the pier railing watching for fish to eat. I released Max's leash so he could be free to run down the pier and chase the birds off of their perch. If it was not for the railing Max would jump off the pier after them as the birds took flight. Hot and tired after clearing the pier of birds Max walked down to the water to cool himself off. I grabbed his leash and coaxed him out of the water so we could finish our walk. After shaking his wet coat all over me we headed back home.

I arrived home to find the front door wide open. I know I closed it before I left. Could someone be waiting for me inside? I looked around cautiously and checked to see if any strange cars were parked on the street or driveway. I slowly walked inside and took off Max's leash. Max raced to his dog bowl in the kitchen to eat. "Hello! Is anyone here?" I yelled. There was no response. I closed and locked the door securely behind me. I convinced myself the wind must have blown the door open.

While Max gobbled down his food, I made myself some pancakes. I was starved for some reason. After breakfast I showered and dressed for church. I always sit with my family during the service. Mom has convinced me I will go to Hell if I dare miss a Sunday at church. I arrived just as the minister was starting to preach and slid into the pew beside my Grandma. My Mom leaned in front of Grandma and gave me the disapproving look that all mothers give their children when they misbehave. She wanted to make sure I knew she was not happy with my late arrival. My mind wandered as the minister spoke and before I knew it he was saying the final prayer. I prepared to sneak out as quickly as possible to avoid my Mom's probing questions. Grandma grabbed my hand as I tried to make my get-away.

"Mildred told me at bingo last night that there is an estate auction in her neighborhood next week. I bet you might find some real treasures for your store."

I knew Grandma was baiting me so I would take her to the sale. "Where is it located and what time do you want me to pick you up?"

"It's on Avocado Way and the auction begins at ten. We better get there early so we can decide what we want to bid on."

43

"Did you say Avocado Way?" That's the same street where Walter Henderson lives, I thought to myself.

"Yes, it's in Pomona Park."

"Do you know the name of the owner whose items are being auctioned?" I pried.

"I believe Mildred said the name was Henderson."

All the color drained from my face.

"Are you feeling okay? You look a little pale."

"Yes, I'm fine. Did Mildred say what happened to Mr. Henderson?"

"Just that he died and all his stuff is being auctioned off."

I started to shake uncontrollably. "I've got to run, Grandma I will see you next weekend," I said as I raced out of the church. I closed my car door, started the engine and cranked the AC to high. I sat there trying to make sense of it all. Could someone have killed Walter Henderson?

Once I arrived home I rushed to log into the Palatka Daily News web site to search the obituaries for Walter Henderson's name. Finally, I found it. Four weeks ago, Walter Henderson died at his home after an extended illness. There was a picture of him. He looked quite distinguished. The picture may have been taken several years ago, but he looked handsome with a sculptured face and muscular frame. I kept reading. He is survived by his son Walter Henderson, Jr. "Maybe his son took the paintings to New York," I thought out loud. I googled Walter Henderson, Jr. to see what I could find. There were several listed. I skimmed through the list and eliminated anyone over the age of forty-five and under the age of twenty. That left four who lived in the Florida area. Maybe he will be at the estate sale on Saturday and I can talk to him about Dorothy's paintings. The phone suddenly rang and I jumped to get it, hoping it was Harper.

"Hi Mom. I'm sorry I lost track of time and forgot about supper. I am not feeling well so I am going to stay home and get some rest." I was just not up to facing my mother and all her questions. I quickly hung up the phone before my mother could make me feel guilty for avoiding her. Max was sitting at my feet staring a hole in me which meant he needed to go out. Some fresh   air would also do me some good. "Okay boy. Let's go for a walk." At hearing the word, "Walk," Max rushed to the door barking with excitement.

It was another sunny, hot, humid summer day in Florida. Thunder clouds were building toward the east in the distance providing a refreshing cool breeze. I walked along the cobblestone path underneath the shade from the large oak trees that lined the street so Max wouldn't get overheated. About a half mile from the house I heard thunder in the distance which meant like most Florida summer afternoons, a storm was not far away. "Sorry boy, we better turn back so we don't get caught in the rain or struck by lightning." A block from home the rain started pouring down. Max and I ran to reach the shelter of my house. The cobblestone quickly became slick from the rain. As I turned to run up the path to my front door, my foot slid out from under me and I fell to the ground. Max licked my face as I sat stunned on the ground, getting drenched from the rain. I evaluated my condition while getting soaked to the bone. It didn't appear as if anything was broken. I suddenly realized the urgency of seeking refuge inside the house as a loud boom shook me to the core. A lightning bolt struck the river, way too close for comfort. Using Max for support, I pushed myself to a standing position and limped into the house. Once inside, I heard the phone ringing and hobbled to the kitchen to answer it.

It was Harper. I explained to him what had just happened and he insisted on coming right over to check on me. I was glad he offered, even though I looked a wreck and my ankle was starting to throb and turn blue.

I found the closest chair and plopped down in it. I dried off the best I could using a kitchen towel and placed some ice on my ankle. It was not long before I heard a frantic knock at the door. It must be Harper. I yelled, "Come in." I heard the door open. "I'm in the kitchen."

"How are you doing?"

"Well, I scraped my elbow and knee, but it's my ankle I'm not too sure about."

Harper lifted the ice pack from my ankle. "That doesn't look good." My ankle had swollen to about twice its normal size. "I better take you to the emergency room to make sure it's not broken. Do you think you can stand?"

"Yes, if you help support me so I can hobble on one leg."

Harper reached down, wrapped his strong arms under my armpits and lifted me to a standing position. He placed my arm around his neck and he held me securely around the waist. "How is that? Do you think you can make it to my truck?"

"Yes, just take it slow." It felt good to have him so close. I held him tightly around his strong shoulders for support and we slowly made our way to his truck without putting weight on my injured ankle. Harper lifted me off the ground and placed me in the seat of his truck as the throbbing in my ankle worsened. On the way to the hospital I filled Harper in on Walter Henderson dying, and that he has a son with the same name.

He agreed, "Since Walter, Sr. is dead it must be the son that's somehow involved in the disappearance of Dorothy's paintings. Do you think it's such a great idea going to the estate auction next Saturday to try to discover more information on the paintings? It could be dangerous."

Before we could discuss it further, Harper pulled up to the emergency room entrance. He ran inside and returned with a wheelchair for me. He once again lifted me out of the truck using his strong arms and wheeled me into the emergency room. After providing my insurance information, I was placed in an exam room, then taken for x-rays.

Harper stayed in the waiting area while I was in x-ray. He rejoined me in the exam room once the x-rays were complete. He comforted me while we waited for the doctor to give me the results. I could see the concern in his eyes. It was nice to have him by my side. The doctor finally appeared with my prognosis.

"It does not appear as if your ankle is broken, but there is a hairline fracture. I am going to put you in a soft cast and give you some crutches to use for a few weeks until the swelling goes down. I don't want you putting any weight on that ankle for at least a week to give the fracture a chance to heal."

Great, I thought to myself. How am I going to take care of everything at the store, and Max, on crutches? After giving me a prescription for pain pills and some anti-inflammatory medicine I was allowed to leave.

"What can I do to help?" Harper asked?

I hated having to rely on someone else and I was not used to being the one who needed help. "I will be fine. I am sure in a few days I will be as good as new again."

"You heard the doctor. He wants you to stay off that ankle. That means no walking. I can start with picking up a pizza for supper tonight. We can figure the rest out from there."

By the time we arrived home the shot the doctor had given me for pain was starting to take affect and all I wanted to do was sleep. I barely remember Harper helping me to bed.

The next morning I woke to a painful light streaming through my bedroom window. I opened my eyes squinting at the brightness. Max's massive head was lying across my chest as he continued to sleep. I dared not move or he would wake up. I slowly lifted my head and looked around the room. Harper was asleep with his arms across his chest in a chair in the corner of the bedroom. I smiled to myself. He was concerned enough about me to stay the night and sleep in an uncomfortable chair. I laid there evaluating my situation. My ankle was throbbing, but not too bad. Since my right ankle was the one injured, I was not going to be able to drive until it was healed. I didn't want to call my Mom for help. I knew she would rush over and in no time be driving me nuts. Maybe I could ask Gloria if she could work extra hours this week and take me to the store. Max stretched his long legs as he slowly came to life. He put his nose up to my face to see if I was awake. I rubbed his head, trying to keep him quiet so as not to

47

wake Harper. Max rolled over on his back so I could rub his tummy. After getting his fill of loving for the morning, Max decided it was time to get up. He jumped off the bed and started to bark. "Shhh!" I tried to keep Max quiet, to no avail.

"What's all the racket? Someone sounds like they are ready to start the day. How are you feeling?"

"Not bad. I slept much better than I am sure you did and my ankle doesn't seem to be too sore. You didn't have to stay the night."

"I know, but I was worried you might wake up once the pain medicine wore off, need something and not be able to get out of bed."

"Thanks for being there for me last night. Can I ask you another favor before you leave for work?"

"Anything, I am at your service," Harper bowed like he was my servant.

"Can you take Max for his morning walk? You will be his best friend forever, for he loves his walks."

"That would be my pleasure, my lady," he answered as he continued to play his role as my servant. "Can I get you anything first before I leave?"

"No, I think I can manage. I see you put my crutches within arms' reach by my bed, so I should be good while you're gone."

"I will leave you madame and return shortly, but first a kiss." Harper leaned down and kissed me jokingly on the lips.

"Don't overdo it while I am gone. Remember the doctor's orders and stay off your feet."

"You're starting to remind me of my mother," I joked as I threw a pillow at him. Max barked to alert Harper as to his urgent need to go out as he waited impatiently.

While Harper was gone I hobbled to the bathroom and looked at myself in the mirror. I was a sight to behold. My hair was sticking straight up in the back and my mascara had run under my eyes, making me look like a raccoon. While leaning on my crutches I quickly took a wash cloth bath, gave up taming my hair

48

and placed it in a ponytail. I washed my face and applied a little makeup. I looked at the results of my effort in the mirror and was satisfied that I wouldn't scare anyone away. I hopped to the kitchen using my good leg and crutches. I opened the refrigerator door and took inventory of what I could fix for breakfast. I had one egg and a little milk. I opened my pantry and found a blueberry muffin mix. I quickly mixed the muffins and placed them in the oven. They needed twenty minutes to cook. I made some coffee while they cooked. Just as my timer went off I heard Harper come through the door with Max leading the way to his food bowl.

"Something smells good."

"Would you like a blueberry muffin and some coffee?"

"Oh, that sounds wonderful! After a quick bite I need to run home, shower and dress for work." Harper devoured his third muffin and gulped down his cup of coffee before grabbing another muffin for the road. "I know your shop is not open today, so I will stop by after work to take Max out to do his business and bring you some food."

"That's not necessary. I know you're busy. I can call Dad to help me today." I protested to no avail.

"It's no trouble, I will see you this evening." Harper rushed out the door before I could say another word.

The house seemed oddly quiet after Harper left. I decided to hold off taking another pain pill to keep my head clear. Standing on one foot I placed the dirty dishes in the sink then collapsed on the sofa and drank another cup of coffee. It was nice being able to count on someone other than myself for a change.

I turned on the TV and found nothing of interest to watch. I was going to go crazy laying around all day, something I am not used to. I eagerly waited for Harper to return with Max keeping me company. With to constant drone of the noise from the TV, I fell asleep. To my surprise, I slept until the sound of Harper knocking on the door woke me.

Harper brought take-out as promised. He picked up BBQ, cold slaw, baked beans, and macaroni and cheese. All my favorites, and I was starved after sleeping all day.

"You're spoiling me rotten. I could get used to this service." I joked with Harper.

During supper Harper explained the plan he had devised for taking care of me. "I will stop by each morning, take Max for a walk, then drop you off at your shop on my way to work. After work I can stop by your shop on my way home, to pick you and Max back up, and take you home."

"I love a man who takes charge, but I don't want to make you late for work. I can have Gloria pick me up."

"Don't be silly. It's on my way and I won't be late. I can flex my hours for a few weeks."

After supper Harper relaxed with me on the sofa. He was so tired from watching over me the night before it was not long before he was sleeping soundly. I watched him sleep and smiled at how nice it was to have him there and how quickly we had become so close. I very quietly covered him with a quilt hanging over the back of the sofa, careful not to wake him. I managed to softly hobble to bed without disturbing him.

***

The next morning I awoke to the smell of coffee and immediately noticed Max was no longer in bed with me. I slowly made my way to the kitchen using my crutches. There was a note on the coffeepot. *Sorry about falling asleep on you last night. Taking Max for a walk. Be back soon.*

I smiled to myself as I poured a cup of coffee. It was nice waking with Harper here with me. I could get used to this, I thought to myself.

I had just sat down when Max stormed through the front door making a beeline to his food dish. "Good morning," Harper said. "How did you sleep?"

"I slept great, amazingly enough since all I did was sit around all day yesterday. How about you?"

"Surprisingly enough, your sofa is very comfortable." Harper leaned over and kissed me gently on the lips. "I've got to run home and change for work, but will be right back to take you to your shop."

Harper reappeared at my door forty-five minutes later dressed in nice slacks and a cotton collared shirt. He loaded Max and me into his truck. Once at the shop he opened the door for me and led Max to his rug behind the register.

"Don't overdo it today. Call me if you need anything. I will be back at six to pick you up."

"I will be fine. Have a good day!" I yelled as he rushed off once again.

Gloria arrived shortly after Harper left. "What in the world happened to you?"

I explained my adventure at the emergency room and how helpful Harper was. All Gloria heard was the Harper portion of the conversation and wanted to know more. I quickly changed the subject.

"I found out Walter Henderson died a little over four weeks ago, so he couldn't have been the one who took Dorothy's paintings."

"Really, well that can't be. The New York gallery said Walter Henderson sold them the paintings."

"I think it must have been Walter Henderson, Jr."

The phone suddenly rang and I reached for the receiver. I whispered to Gloria, "It's Audrey." Audrey shared the information she had found on Walter Henderson from the tax records.

"Mr. Henderson's last place of employment was the wood processing plant. It appears he retired about five years ago. His income dropped significantly after that. He didn't renew his vehicle registration this year."

"That's probably because he died," I added.

"Well, I was getting to that. It looks like his estate filed a notice to make his debtors aware of his demise," Audrey added.

"Can you look up Walter Henderson, Jr. and let me know what you find?" I asked.

"Hang on."

I heard the computer keys clicking.

"Walter, Jr. does not appear to currently have a job and was arrested for drug possession a few years ago. He is currently out of jail and his last know vehicle was an older model Ford Mustang."

"Interesting. Thanks for the information. Are you planning to come to quilters club on Friday night?"

"I wouldn't miss it. I've got to run. Bye."

"So what did she say?" Gloria anxiously asked.

I looked over my notes from my conversation with Audrey. "Walter Henderson worked at the same wood processing plant as Herman Evanston, Dorothy's husband."

"Maybe they were friends," Gloria added.

"They might have been. They would have both been about the same age. I just cannot believe that Dorothy would willingly give her paintings to him, though."

"Maybe he needed the money for medical treatments and that was Dorothy's way of helping."

"That's possible, I guess. Oh, and Audrey also told me that Walter's son is currently unemployed and had been arrested for drug possession. So maybe his son figures into this somehow. It looks like he could have definitely needed the money."

"Kids nowadays. They all seem to be so self absorbed and into drugs." Gloria realized that Maggie was just a kid, "I mean, not you of course. I don't think of you as a kid. Your Mom raised you right, hard working, and considerate of others."

"Thanks Gloria, I knew what you meant."

Gloria waited until Harper arrived before she left for the day. She said she wanted to make sure I had a way home, but I really think she just wanted to spy on me.

Harper's truck pulled in front of the store right at six. Gloria gave me a wicked smile and walked to the door.

"You two stay out of trouble this evening, you hear?"

Max ran to greet Harper as soon as he entered the store. "Well, you have definitely made a new friend."

"I'm sure he just needs to pee and sees me as the person to take him for a walk. I'll take him to the closest tree and be right back."

While Harper was busy with Max, I leaned on my crutches and turned off the store lights, flicked off the open sign, and locked the door.

Harper helped Max and me into his truck then suggested, "How about we stop by the The Diner to get some burgers, fries, and a chocolate milkshake on the way home?"

"That sounds delicious and just what I need after sitting around all day, tons of fat and calories," I joked.

"Max, I am sure you wouldn't mind a burger for supper tonight." Max barked on cue, answering with a definite yes.

# Seven

After hurting my ankle on Sunday, I managed to make it through the rest of the week without any more unusual incidents. The house had been quiet and there were no unexplainable noises, thankfully. Harper continued to come by each morning, take Max for a walk, drop him off at my shop, and stop by after work each day to drive us home. I was enjoying being spoiled by Harper and spending time with him every day. I could get used to having him around.

By Saturday morning when the estate auction was planned, my ankle had returned to its normal size. The swelling had gone down considerably and I could get around using the soft cast without the crutches. After telling Grandma about my ankle she agreed to drive us to the estate auction. She had an old four door Buick with faded blue paint that sat most of the time in my Dad's garage. I hoped I was not going to regret accepting Grandma's offer to drive. I was rummaging through the clutter in my garage for a couple of folding chairs when I heard Grandma pull up in front of the house and impatiently honk the horn.

As I slowly made my way to the car with the chairs Grandma yelled, "Hurry up so we don't miss out on anything!"

"I'm walking as fast as I can!" I yelled back. "What's the big hurry? The auction doesn't start for another hour, so we have plenty of time. Open your trunk so I can put these chairs inside."

Grandma searched for a trunk release lever to no avail. "Just throw them in the back seat," she hollered out the window.

Once inside the car, Grandma hurriedly put the car in gear as I fastened my seat belt. When we reached Main Street she squealed her tires as she pulled out in front of another car. I held onto the door for dear life and waited for the impact. After some horn blowing, where I thought road rage may be our demise, we were on our way. The AC was broken in the car so the windows were down to keep the air moving. I held my hair back with my hand to keep it from blowing in my face. We managed to make it to our destination in one piece. There was already a line of cars parked down the street so Grandma parked behind the last car. I slowly got out of the car, grateful to be on solid ground. Grandma took off toward the house, ahead of me.

Furniture and general household goods lined the driveway to Walter's house. I rummaged through what was being auctioned and saw little of any great value. You could tell Walter was not an extravagant man. The furniture looked to be thirty years old and the kitchen items not much newer. When I reached the end of the driveway, I noticed the front door of the house was open. Curiosity got the best of me and I peered inside. The house looked empty except for a few boxes stacked along the back wall of the living room. I noticed what looked to be a painting sticking out of one of the boxes. I crept inside and looked in the box. It was one of Dorothy's paintings. I picked it up and was amazed at what I saw. It was a painting of a man holding a fishing pole in one hand and a large bass in the other with a big smile across his face. I smiled back, thinking of all the times my Dad was that happy after catching a big bass.

"That painting is not part of the auction."

I quickly turned around, realizing I had been caught. "I'm sorry I didn't mean to intrude. This is such an expressive painting. You can feel the emotion this man must have felt."

"That was my father. He loved to fish."

"Do you know the artist?" I played dumb. "I would love to buy one of her paintings."

"My father knew her well. After my Mom died my father was lost. He ran into Dorothy during her husband's funeral a few years ago. Since they had both lost their spouses, they became close and often kept each other company. Then my Dad was diagnosed with cancer and Dorothy passed away suddenly. My

Dad was heartbroken for a second time. He seemed to lose his will to live. It was not long after Dorothy died that he lost his battle with cancer."

"Such a sad story. I didn't mean to pry. The artist definitely had talent. Do you know if she created any other paintings before she passed away?" I continued to probe.

"I imagine she did, but I don't know what happened to them after her death."

He has got to be lying. There is no way his father could have taken them to New York. I heard the auctioneer calling out for bids. I placed the painting of Walter back in the box where I had found it. "I'm sorry for your loss." I turned and went back outside.

I searched the crowd for Grandma and then heard her yell out, "Ten dollars!" What in the world is she bidding on? I looked toward the auctioneer and saw a box of miscellaneous goods being auctioned. Before I could reach Grandma I heard, "Sold to the lady in the yellow hat!"

Dad is going to kill me for letting Grandma buy something. I made my way through the crowd and reached Grandma before she could bid on anything else. "Why did you bid on that box? It appears to be filled with nothing but junk."

"No one was bidding. No telling what kind of treasures could be in that box."

I rolled my eyes. "Grandma, you know Dad does not have any more room to store your stuff."

"I bought it for you. I am sure there will be something in the box you can sell at your store."

I felt bad for scolding her. What else could I say but, "Thank you, that was thoughtful of you."

I bid on an antique hope chest but gave up when the bid reached fifty dollars. So, other than Grandma's box of junk, we left the auction with what we came with. Grandma dropped me off at the store. I set the box Grandma bought on the counter.

"What do we have here?" Gloria asked?

"Grandma bought this at the auction thinking it may have something inside we could sell in the store."

"It doesn't look too promising." Gloria said as she peered inside the box and started removing items. I watched as she removed some worn pot holders, dish towels, a rusted pair of scissors and an old rusted cookie tin. Gloria shook the cookie tin and something rattled inside. She pried off the lid.

"What is it?" I eagerly asked.

"It appears to be an envelope." Gloria reached inside the cookie tin and pulled out the envelope and reached inside it. She removed a piece of paper and carefully unfolded it. "This is interesting. It looks like a letter from Dorothy to Walter."

"You're kidding?" I hurried over to look at it. "Notice the date on top of the page. This was written a week before Dorothy died."

Chills ran down my spine as I reached for the letter. I read the letter out loud.

"*Walter, When you and Herman were working on the logging road, many years ago, Herman discovered some buried treasure. You had left with the logging truck to deliver a load to the plant when Herman got the tractor stuck in the mud. He started digging in the muck so he could put something under the tire to help get some traction, when he noticed something shiny in the dirt. He picked it up and discovered a dirty Spanish coin. He dug around the area some more and found some bones and three more Spanish coins. Herman brought the coins home with him that night and showed them to me. He was scared to tell anyone about the coins or bones he found for fear it would shut down operations in the area. If anyone knew, they might deem it an archaeological site. Now that Herman is gone, I want you to know where he hid the Spanish coins. He always felt bad about not sharing them with you. To keep the coins safe he buried them. The secret to where the coins are hidden is in the wildflower painting by the river, with the flowers I loved so much. Leave no stone*

57

unturned. *If something happens to me, unbury the coins, sell them, and use the money for yourself."*

"My word, Maggie. Your house may have buried treasure in it!"

"What does she mean, in the wildflower painting by the river? I don't remember any of Dorothy's paintings being of wildflowers by the river. Do you think Walter found the coins?"

"I doubt it. You said that Walter's health declined quickly after Dorothy passed away. He may not have been physically able to unbury them." Gloria thought for a second then asked, "Do you think Walter, Sr., told his son, about the letter? Maybe that's why he took the paintings."

"Now that's a good question and may explain why someone has been snooping around my house. Today at the auction I found a painting of Walter, Sr. that Dorothy had painted, in a box inside Walter's house. I guess her and Walter became close after Herman passed away."

"That would explain why she wrote the letter to Walter. She trusted him enough to know he wouldn't tell."

"Well, maybe. I asked Walter, Jr. today if he knew if Dorothy had created other paintings and he replied that he didn't know. I know Walter, Jr. had to have taken Dorothy's paintings to New York, so why did he lie to me?"

"Maybe because he didn't have permission and stole the paintings."

"If that was the case, you would think Walter, Jr., would have gotten enough money from the sale of the paintings to buy a new car. He's driving a beat up Mustang."

"What are you going to do?"

"Well, I'm going to try to figure out the riddle in the letter of the wildflower painting by the river that Dorothy refers to and see if the coins are still where Herman buried them."

The bell above the door jingled as a customer entered the store. I looked up to see Mabel, the town gossip. I whispered to

Gloria, "Don't share what we have found." I hurriedly placed the letter and contents of the box behind the counter.

"How are you doing today, Mabel?" Gloria cheerfully greeted her.

"Did you hear there was another burglary in my neighborhood this week? I swear I don't know what this town is coming to. I used to sleep with my windows open and doors unlocked, but not any more."

"I know what you mean. You cannot be too careful these days."

"Can I help you find something Mabel, or is this just a social visit?" I asked.

Mabel looked around the store to see if anything interested her, "No, I don't need anything. I just stopped by to say hi. I heard you and Sylvia's brother are seeing each other. Are there any wedding bells in the future?" Mabel pried.

"No, we are just friends." It sounded strange coming from my lips. I'm not sure I believed we were just friends any more. But what were we?

I looked up to see Harper walking down the street toward the store. I didn't want to have to explain our relationship to Mabel any further. "Well, Mabel it was nice seeing you today." I walked her to the door and opened it for her. Thank goodness she took the hint. She turned and walked the opposite direction from Harper.

I motioned for Harper to quickly step inside the store before Mabel saw him.

"Okay, who are you trying to hide me from?"

"You should thank me. That was Mabel, the town gossip. If I had let her see you she would be pelting you with questions about us, where you work, what are your plans for the future, are you planning to have a large family, and on and on. You never would have heard the end of it."

"Well, thanks for coming to my rescue."

59

"What are you doing here so early? I don't close the store for another three hours."

"I know. I was in the area and just thought I would stop by. I wanted to see if you had returned from the auction yet and see how your ankle was holding up."

"That was so considerate of you. My ankle is holding up, as you can see." I held out my leg and showed Harper that I still had on the boot to protect my ankle.

Gloria spoke up, "All right you love birds. If Harper is going to stay I need to leave early to run some errands."

I rolled my eyes at Gloria, "Thanks for your help today. I will see you on Tuesday."

After Gloria left, I filled Harper in on my conversation with Walter, Jr., on finding the letter and the possible hidden treasure. "What do you think the clue in the wildflower painting by the river means?"

"No telling. It could have been in reference to something Dorothy and Walter had experienced together, not necessarily something she painted."

"I hadn't considered that. You know, it's going to drive me nuts until I figure it out."

"How about I take you out to dinner tonight and we can work on the puzzle together?"

"That sounds nice." I leaned over and gave Harper a kiss. "Do you mind helping me until the store closes? I hate to admit it, but my ankle is starting to ache and I should probably get off my feet for a little while."

"I was afraid you would over do it today. Just let me know what you need."

"I received an order of silk flowers yesterday. Can you unbox them for me and set them on the counter so I can arrange and price them?" I kept Harper busy the rest of the afternoon. After work we dropped Max off at the house and Harper took me to a local fish house to eat. We sat by the river enjoying our meal, listening to a local band play, and watched the sun set. I felt so relaxed in his company. Harper and I talked the night away.

When Harper and I arrived home the front door was wide open. I ran through the house yelling, "Max, come boy." I heard whining coming from the bedroom closet. I looked inside my closet and found Max hiding underneath my clothes hanging on the rack. "Are you all right? Did someone scare you?" I gave Max a big hug and buried my face in Max's coat.

While I comforted Max, Harper called the police to report the break in. An officer quickly arrived and pulled up to the front of my house.

"We have had a rash of break-ins lately. Do you have a list of what was taken?"

"Well, that's the strange thing. I can't find anything missing."

The officer examined the door. "It doesn't look like the lock was tampered with. Does anyone else have a key to your house?"

"No, I just changed the locks. I dropped Max off just after six and all appeared normal."

"Do you have any idea who would have known you wouldn't be home?"

"Well, just about anyone that knows I have a store and work there during the day, but no one knew I had plans to go out tonight."

"Any idea what they may have been looking for?"

Dorothy's letter to Walter entered my mind. "No, I have no idea. I've only lived in the house about a month."

"Well, I'll have the officers make additional drive by's in this area to keep an eye out for anyone suspicious, but that's probably the best we can do until we have more info."

"I understand. Thanks for your help."

After the officer left, I remembered that the front door was open after my walk with Max a couple of days ago. I pulled on the front door to make sure it latched securely when it was closed. It didn't budge.

61

Harper watched me with a worried look on his face, "I'm not going to leave you alone tonight just in case the intruder decides to come back."

I didn't want to worry Harper, so I didn't mention the other incident involving the front door. "You've been coming to my rescue a lot lately. What could I ever do to repay you?" I rolled my eyes giving Harper my innocent look.

"I'm sure I can think of something." Harper leaned down and kissed me passionately. The kissing continued and it was not long before we ended up in bed making love.

In the middle of the night I suddenly woke. I heard the sound of footsteps in the attic again. I looked at the clock and it was 3AM. Harper had his arms wrapped securely around me. I decided not to disturb him and gently lifted his arm off my stomach and slid from the bed. Max was sound asleep at the foot of the bed and didn't stir. I grabbed the flashlight on the night stand and walked to the attic stairs. Once in the attic I turned on the flashlight and pointed it toward the easel by the window. Dorothy's ghost was sitting there as before, but the unfinished painting was gone. I tried to remain calm so Dorothy would show me what she has been trying to communicate. Dorothy floated up from the chair and went to the window.

"Maggie, you up there?" I heard Harper yell.

"Damn!" Dorothy disappeared again before she could tell me what was troubling her. "Yes, I'll be right down." I crawled down the ladder, being careful not to re-injure my ankle.

"What are you doing in the attic at 3AM?"

"I heard a noise and went to investigate. The unfinished painting on the easel is gone." I decided it would be best not to tell Harper about seeing Dorothy's ghost again. With everything that has happened lately I am sure he would think I've totally lost it.

"Did you look around the attic to see if it just fell off the easel?"

"No, it was too dark. Let's go back to bed and I'll return in the morning when there is more light."

We crawled back into bed and Harper snuggled against me, wrapping his arms gently around my chest so I could not get up without waking him. He fell fast asleep and I laid there listening to him breathe deeply in and out while I tried to figure out what Dorothy was trying to show me. The first time I saw her she pointed toward the painting of the view out the window and this time she was trying to show me something outside the window. What was she needing me to see? Before my mind could figure it out I drifted off to sleep. I awoke to Max breathing in my face. I rolled over and bumped into Harper. I had forgotten he was in bed beside me.

"Good morning."

"I'm sorry, I didn't mean to wake you."

He rolled over to give me a hug and Max started to bark.

"This is Max's time of the day and I think he is jealous."

"It's okay, boy. I'll get up and take you for a walk before it gets too hot." Harper had been taking Max for a walk ever since I hurt my ankle. I think they both enjoyed their morning walks.

As if Max understood, he ran to the front door. Harper threw on shorts and a t-shirt he kept at my house and left to walk Max. I took advantage of the time alone and quickly showered and started some coffee. Memories of what had happened in the attic last night came back to me. I had to know if the painting was truly gone. I grabbed the flashlight and headed back to the attic. Once at the top of the stairs, I looked around and everything appeared in order except the painting was still not on the easel. I noticed an object in the far dark corner of the attic that I hadn't seen before. The roof line made it difficult to reach, so I crawled on my hand and knees until I reached the object. The painting that had been on the easel was laying against what appeared to be an old hope chest. I lifted the painting off the chest and wondered how it mysteriously moved from the easel. I set the painting on the floor beside the chest. I examined the wooden box in front of me. Even through the dust I could see it was well crafted. I moved the painting back to the easel then returned to the hope chest on my hands and knees. I needed to move the chest to the center of the attic so I could open it and see what was inside. The handles were made from heavy rope, like what is used to secure a boat to a dock. I tested the sturdiness of the rope handles to make sure they hadn't degraded with age. The rope appeared to be in good shape and not rotted. I tugged harder and carefully dragged the hope chest across the floor, inches at a time, as I scooted along in front of it. Out of breath, sweaty, and hot I reached the center of the attic where the ceiling was high enough for me to stand. I brushed the dust from the top. The woodwork was magnificent. The chest appeared to be made of old cypress planks. The wood grain weaved through the top and sides with a multitude of colors and patterns. I ran my hand over the wood's grain and felt the smooth polished finish. I slowly lifted the lid to see what was inside. My eyes were delighted to find a beautiful quilt carefully folded inside. It must have been an heirloom from Dorothy's family. I gently removed it, being careful not to get it dirty. The quilt was made up of individual squares of wildflowers meticulously hand sewn in place. Each stitch the same length as the next. It must have taken someone years to complete this quilt. I heard Max and Harper come through the front door. I yelled down, "I'm in the attic. Can you join me up here?"

Next, I heard a series of thuds as Harper climbed the ladder.

"Look what I found!" delighted with myself.

"Wow, that's gorgeous, which meant a lot coming from a man that knows little about quilts."

"It must be close to one hundred years old. Can you help me get the chest out of the attic?" I laid the quilt back inside.

"I thought you said the painting was not in the easel last night?"

"The strangest thing, I found it laying against this chest way back there in the corner of the attic. I placed it back on the easel."

"Could whoever broke into the house yesterday have moved it?"

"Why would they do that? Don't you think if someone found the painting they would have taken it?"

"I guess you're right. They wouldn't have just moved it."

"Help me push the chest to the attic door."

Harper pulled while I pushed the chest toward the stairwell opening. He stopped at the top of the stairs and climbed part way down so the chest was at shoulder height. "Hold your end so it won't fall on top of my head, and slowly lower it down to me."

"Okay, let me know when you're ready for me to begin pushing it your way."

"I'm ready. Slowly push it toward me and I will hold it as it slides down the stairs."

Without too much trouble the chest now lay at the bottom of the stairs. I opened the lid and pulled out the quilt once again to get a better look at it.

"Don't you think it's strange the quilt is of wildflowers? It's just like the reference in the letter I found to Walter of the wildflower painting by the river."

"Dorothy must have liked wildflowers." Harper quickly dismissed my observation.

"I need to take a quick shower. Would you like to join me?" He grabbed me by the arm and brought me to his chest, lifting my face to his, and kissed me.

I placed my hand on Harper's chest and pushed him back. "No more kissing until you smell a little better."

"Okay, I can take a hint. Walking Max can be sweaty business."

Harper pulled off his t-shirt, showing his muscular body, and headed to the bathroom as I smiled to myself. He was awful hard to resist. I returned to the kitchen to finish making pancakes for breakfast.

"Something smells wonderful," Harper said as he appeared in the kitchen with a starved looked. He placed several pancakes on his plate and covered them in syrup.

"I love a man with a huge appetite like mine," I joked.

The phone rang just as we started to eat our pancakes. "Hello. Hi Mom." I looked at Harper and rolled my eyes. "No, I'm going to skip church this morning. I've had a busy week and need to rest." I just hoped God would forgive me for lying to my mother. "Dinner? Yes, I know I missed last week. I know you want to meet Harper. I will give him a call and see if he is free and let you know. Goodbye Mother." I had hoped to hold out as long as possible before Harper met my family. There was no telling what kind of questions my Mom and Grandma would ask. I'm sure they will embarrass me to no avail.

"Sounds like we have a dinner invitation."

"We don't have to go if you would rather do something else."

"No, I would like to meet your parents. You should call your Mom back and let her know we are coming."

"Okay, but I've got to warn you, my mother can go just a little bit overboard. She will interrogate you, and no matter how great you are, she will find a flaw."

"I gather no one is good enough for her little girl."

"Well there is that, but mostly she is in a hurry to get me married and provide her with grandchildren. So don't be surprised if she asks you if you want to have a large family."

"That will be easy to answer. I love children and hope to have some of my own one day." Harper's deep blue eyes twinkled as he looked into mine.

"Really?"

"Why do you sound surprised?"

"Most guys your age who have just gotten out of college and started a career want to wait until they have had time to enjoy their freedom, that's all."

Harper leaned over and gave me a kiss. "If you haven't figure it out yet, I am not like most guys."

I climbed into Harpers lap and kissed him deeply, enjoying the taste of syrup from his lips. "We have a few hours before we have to be at my parents. I wonder what we could do to occupy our time?"

Harper carried me into the bedroom and hurriedly closed the door before Max could come barreling in on us.

# Eight

Dinner with my family is never dull, to say the least. We arrived at one o'clock to the sounds of my Mom yelling at Grandma to not eat all the dessert. I cautiously entered the house. Dad was in the living room relaxing in his recliner, reading the paper, ignoring the commotion in the kitchen.

"Hi, Dad. I would like you to meet Harper."

"Nice to meet you, Harper." Dad said gruffly.

"Dad, Harper enjoys fishing." I hoped that would give them something to talk about.

"After getting skunked the last time we went out, I'm ready to try again," Dad said.

"What did you use for bait?" Harper asked.

"We normally use shiners, but the bass just weren't interested this week."

"I've got this new lure I just bought that's supposed to be the latest craze for catching large mouth bass," Harper added.

While Dad and Harper talked fishing, I quietly crept into the kitchen to referee Mom and Grandma.

"Look who finally decided to show up!" Mom said.

"Mom, it hasn't been that long, and I've been busy."

"What did you do to your ankle? Why didn't you call and let me know you were injured? You look skinny as a rail. Have you been eating?"

I peeled Mom off the ceiling and reminded her, "I am a grown woman, and believe it or not, my parents raised me so I could take care of myself. I am fine. I just twisted my ankle walking Max. Something smells delicious. What are we having for dinner?"

"Your favorite of course, lasagna with extra cheese, garlic bread, salad and cheesecake for dessert. Where is this boyfriend of yours?"

"He's in the living room talking to Dad. Can I help set the table?"

"Yes, it's nice to have help for a change." Mom glared at Grandma.

I set the table and then helped Mom carry the delicious smelling food to the table.

"All right guys, dinner is ready," Mom yelled into the living room.

"Harper, it's nice to finally meet you. I would tell you I've heard so many nice things about you, but my daughter does not talk to her mother anymore."

"Well, aren't you a handsome one," Grandma chimed in. "You can sit over here next to me." Grandma motioned for Harper to sit in the chair beside her.

Harper was polite and charmed my Mom and Grandma throughout the meal. Just as I predicted, Mom went out of her way to embarrass me.

"Maggie grew up a tomboy with her hair in pigtails, wearing cut-off jeans and t-shirts. She was never interested in dolls or wearing dresses. When she became a teenager I worried she would never date. No guy would find her attractive enough."

Harper spoke up in my defense, "I can't imagine Maggie back then. She is always dressed nice and is so beautiful."

I looked at Harper and smiled. He thinks I am beautiful, I thought to myself. After two torturous hours we finished the cheesecake for dessert and I helped clean the kitchen. "Mom, I hate to eat and run, but Harper has agreed to help me with some repairs around the house." Harper just didn't know it yet.

"Let me send you home with some left overs so you will have something to eat tonight."

"Thanks, Mom."

Mom thrust a bag full of disposable dishes filled with food at me.

"It was nice meeting you all," Harper graciously said as I grabbed his hand and led him in the direction of the car.

On the drive home I congratulated Harper on how well he answered all of my Mom's questions. "I think you passed inspection today. Thanks for being so nice to my family. I know they can be difficult."

"Just be happy that my Mom lives in Georgia or you would be going through the same scrutiny."

"I don't know anything about your family now that you mention it. I obviously know Sylvia is your sister, but she never talks about your parents. I guess I figured it was none of my business."

"Well, she probably didn't say much because our Dad died from lung cancer about ten years ago. Sylvia helped raise me while mom worked two jobs to take care of us. Mom managed to save enough for only one of us to go to college. I was very fortunate that Sylvia sacrificed her education for me. After all my Mom did for me she is very protective of her little boy."

"I can't wait to meet her. She sounds like a very strong woman."

"Now that you mention it, you have some of her same qualities. You're both strong willed and hard working."

"I think that's a compliment. Thanks."

"Yes, I love that about you. Like finding you in the attic at 3AM. My mother would never hesitate to do something on her own and would rather not ask for help."

"I guess I was raised to be independent, but I am glad you have been around to lean on lately. Which reminds me, can you stop by the hardware store on the way home so I can pick up some light bulbs and a new ceiling fan for the porch? It would be nice to have an operational fan on the screened porch so we can sit outside in comfort."

"No problem. If you're nice to me I will even help you install it." Harper laughed.

"How did I get so lucky?" I leaned over and kissed Harper on the cheek.

Harper helped pick out a fan and we headed to check out at the register. The total came to just under one hundred dollars. I ran my charge card through the machine.

"I'm sorry. Your charge card has been declined."

"How can that be? I know I am not over my limit. I'll just write a check."

We arrived home, to the delight of Max. Harper took him out to do his business while I immediately contacted my credit card company.

After going through several minutes of menu options on the phone I finally reached a person to talk to at the credit card company. "I tried to use my credit card today, but it was declined. I just made a payment, so I know I am not over my limit. No, I haven't made any purchases at a liquor store or bought a new TV lately. You think someone stole my credit card? You're going to freeze my account? Okay, thanks for your help."

Harper returned with Max panting up a storm from the heat. I turned to him, "They are going to issue me a new credit card. My credit card number appears to have been stolen. Can you believe that?"

"Maybe that's what was taken on Saturday when we arrived home and found the door open."

"I guess that's possible, but why only steal the charge card number and nothing else in the house?"

"Easy cash I guess. It's unreal the length people will go to today to get what they want without having to work for it. Now that you have taken care of that, show me where you want this ceiling fan hung."

After getting Max some water, I scrounged up the few tools we needed, and a ladder. Harper and I worked well together. I was able to anticipate what tool he needed before he asked, and the fan was installed in no time. Harper pulled the cord on the fan and the blades of the fan spun around rapidly, providing the breeze needed to cool us off. Hot and sweaty, we both collapsed on the porch lounge chairs underneath the fan.

"Ahhh, this is nice! I'll grab us something to drink and be right back."

I quickly returned with two large glasses of sweet tea. The sun was just starting to set and I admired the view toward the river. The water sparkled as the sun sank below the horizon. My mind wandered to the painting in the attic, capturing the serene view in front of me. Dorothy had managed to bring the river to life in her painting. I was brought out of my daydream at the sound of Harper's voice.

"How about giving the sweaty handy man a hug and kiss for all his hard work?" Harper grabbed me giving me a bear hug so I couldn't squirm away. He jokingly kissed me all over.

"How about I heat up some of Mom's left overs for supper?"

"That sounds good. After we eat it should be cool enough to take Max for a short walk."

I returned with two plates of food and placed them on the patio table. Even though my house is not directly on the river, I have a view of the river from my front porch. I enjoy sitting outside watching the different boats navigating down the waterway. The St. Johns River is one of the few rivers that flows north and ends in Jacksonville, exiting into the ocean. Since it's connected to the ocean and large lakes such as Lake George, all size boats can be seen navigating down it. You never know what you may watch float by. Tonight a thirty plus foot cabin cruiser was slowly making it's way down the river. Being Sunday, I imagined they were headed home after having a fun day in the springs. I dreamed one day of owning my own boat. I imagined how nice it would be to take a slow, leisurely cruise up and down the river to explore the many sights along the way. There are several restaurants along the river that provide a dock to secure your boat while you eat and then you can continue on your way enjoying the sights on the river.

As if Harper could read my mind he asked, "Have you ever thought about buying a boat?"

"Yes, I definitely have that on my bucket list of things to experience in my lifetime. I love everything having to do with the outdoors and would love spending time relaxing on the river with you." I hoped Harper didn't think me too presumptuous including him in my future plans.

He squeezed my hand and leaned over to kiss me. "That does sound nice."

Max started barking wildly to remind us after being cramped up in the house all day he was ready for his evening walk. "All right Max, how about we walk to the park and play ball?" The park was just a block away so I could easily manage with my bum ankle.

Harper added, "I could also use a walk after all that food!" He poked out his tummy showing how full he was. He grabbed Max's leash and hooked it to the collar of one overly energetic dog. We slowly made our way to the park.

The evening was nice with a gentle breeze blowing across the water. The setting sun lit up the horizon with an orange hue. I made myself comfortable on the park bench while Harper threw the ball for Max. Max was ever so loyal. No matter where the ball ended up, he would always retrieve it, squish it between his jaws a couple of times then return it to Harper, dropping it at his feet to throw again.

"All right, one last throw then we better go home. It's getting dark and the mosquitos are starting to bite," Harper told Max.

Harper held the ball up for Max to see then leaned back and threw it as far as he could. Unfortunately, it hit a palm tree about fifty feet in front of us and bounced into the water. Max dove in after the ball.

"Come on Max, I know you love the water, but it's time to go home." Max climbed onto the shore and shook himself dry when I noticed something other than a tennis ball in his mouth. "What do you have there? Drop it," I commanded.

Max obeyed and laid the object on the ground by my feet. That's when I fainted. I awoke to Harper gently slapping me on the face and calling out my name.

"Maggie, wake up! Are you all right?"

Then I remembered why I had fainted. "Did Max retrieve what I think he did?"

"If you mean a hand, then yes. I called the police and they are on their way. How are you feeling? Can you stand?"

Before I could answer, Harper lifted me to a standing position. "Just rest on the bench while we wait for the police to arrive."

While the color returned to my face, I got another glimpse of the hand lying on the ground where Max had dropped it. Harper handed me Max's leash so I could keep him restrained. "Oh, my gosh! Whose hand could it be, where is the rest of their body, and how did it end up in the river?"

"All good questions and I am sure the police will also want the answers to them."

The same officer who was at my house the previous night was the first on the scene. Harper and I explained how the hand ended up on the shore. The officer secured the scene placing crime scene tape around several trees to keep people away from the body part. Several more officers arrived, all wanting to see the hand while they waited for the medical examiner. Harper sat next to me on the park bench. I was in disbelief as my imagination conjured up all kinds of possibilities of how a hand became disconnected from its body. It could have been sawed off and thrown into the river, torn off by an alligator, boating accident... the possibilities were endless.

The medical examiner and scuba team arrived. It was now dark and I watched as the diver's bright lights illuminated the

74

water around them as they searched underwater for the rest of the body. The medical examiner placed the hand in a bag, then sealed and labeled it.

Even though the night was warm I felt chilled, and wrapped my arms around myself trying to stop shaking. Max lay at my feet as if sensing something was wrong.

"Are you cold?" Harper placed his arms around me. "I'll ask the officer if they are done with us so we can go home."

I watched as Harper exchanged words with one of the police officers, not able to hear what they were saying. Harper returned and placed his supporting arm around my shoulders. "Let's go home. The officer has no more questions for us for now and will contact us as needed."

Harper took Max's leash from me and I walked home still in a daze at what I had seen. I was just numb. I didn't feel anything, but extreme fatigue. We entered the house and Harper handed me a pill and a glass of water.

"Take this, it will help you sleep."

I obeyed like a robot. Harper took the glass from me, set it on the counter, then helped me to bed. That's the last thing I remembered until I awoke, still groggy, to a room ablaze with light. I looked at the clock. It read 9:00. Oh my gosh, I never sleep that late! I jumped out of bed and tripped over Max, trying to stay cool, sleeping on the floor by my bed. "I'm sorry Max, I didn't see you." I reached down, gently patted Max on the head to let him know I didn't mean to kick him. I walked into the kitchen, following the smell of coffee. There was a note on the refrigerator door. *"You were sleeping so soundly I didn't want to wake you before I left for work. Max has been walked and fed. Call me when you get up."*

I reached for the coffeepot and poured a cup of coffee. I smiled to myself as I inhaled the coffee. "Harper is so good to me. I am the luckiest girl in the world." The store was closed on Mondays so I had the day to myself. I had a doctors appointment after lunch so the doctor could examine my ankle to determine how it was healing. The fourth of July was only five days away.

The town was planning a big celebration with a fireworks display. The fireworks are launched from a barge on the St. Johns River after dark. There is also music and vendors selling food. I hoped the holiday would attract some tourists to my shop to increase my sales for the month. I decided to work on a window display for the store to help advertise and bring in more customers. I discussed my plans with Max since he was the only one at home. "I will make a big banner with stars and stripes announcing my fourth of July sale. How does that sound, Max?" Max barked as if he understood. "I can place some red, white, and blue balloons outside the entrance of the store to attract some attention."

I felt rested for the first time in weeks. The memory of last night slowly came back to me. "Max, I wonder whether the police have identified who the hand you found belongs to yet." Before my pleasant mood was spoiled, Max barked to remind me he needed to go out. "All right, let me get your leash."

I walked outside and the first thing I saw down the street at the park was a line of television news trucks. The Jacksonville television stations must have heard about finding the body part and were reporting live from the scene about a possible gory death. It repulsed me to see the news media taking advantage of someone's misfortune, filming at the scene like vultures. Don't they realize that the hand could belong to someone's brother or father whose loved ones are waiting to hear from him? I turned to walk in the opposite direction when I ran into my neighbor.

"Did you hear they found a body in the river?"

I didn't feel like correcting her that it was only a hand. "Yes, it's truly awful."

Max quickly did his business and I retreated to the safety of my home. My mood and appetite were now spoiled. I pulled out some art supplies and started working on the fourth of July banner for the store. The phone suddenly rang and I remembered I forgot to call Harper. He is probably wondering why I haven't called.

"Hello. Yes, I'm fine. I'm sorry. I got busy working on a window display for my store and forgot to call." I hung up with a smile on my face. Talking to Harper always cheered me up. He was so considerate to call to make sure I was doing okay after what I had seen last night. Harper is not like any of the other guys I had dated. I feel like I can tell him anything. In just a few short weeks we had grown closer than any of my previous relationships.

Before I realized it, several hours had passed and it was lunch time. Max was barking to remind me it was past time to eat. I could set my watch by Max's stomach. "Where did the morning go, boy?" Max's bark became more insistent. "All right, I'm coming!" I scooped a cup of dry dog food and placed it in Max's food dish. I looked at my watch. I've just enough time to shower and change before my one o'clock doctor's appointment.

I took my boot off just long enough to drive to the doctor's office then placed it back on in the parking lot so the doctor wouldn't give me a lecture. I had barely taken a seat in the waiting room when the nurse called my name.

After taking another x-ray and feeling around my ankle the doctor announced, "I've got good news. It appears the fracture is healing well. There is no swelling, the color is good which means you have good circulation. I want you to wear the boot for one more week and then you can remove it."

"Thank you, doc. That's the best news I've heard all day. This boot is not particularly cool. It will feel so good to have it off."

"Don't go trying to run a marathon once the boot is removed. Take it easy for a few weeks to let your muscles strengthen in that leg."

On the way home from the doctor, I stopped at my shop to place the decorations in the window for the fourth of July. I attached the large banner in the upper part of the window announcing a big sale. Then I sprinkled some red, white, and blue confetti underneath the banner. I hung several red, white, and blue streamers and balloons in the window. I walked outside, stood back and admired my work, pleased with myself. Well, that should attract some attention, I thought.

77

I hurried home to make a special supper for Harper. I opened the door and immediately noticed Max was not waiting for me. That's strange. "Here, Max. Come, boy." When I didn't receive a response I knew immediately that something was wrong. I raced to the kitchen and came to a sudden stop. A gun was pointed at my face.

"It's about time you got home."

I couldn't believe my eyes. It was Walter, Jr. I glanced at Walter's arm and saw a bloody bandage where his hand should be. I tried to remain calm. "Walter, what do you want?"

"I want the coins that belong to my Dad."

"I don't know what you're talking about."

"Don't lie to me," he angrily responded. "I know why you were asking about Dorothy's painting at the estate auction on Saturday."

"Walter, you don't look good. What happened to your hand? Can I get you a doctor?"

"I had a little problem when someone I owe money to came to collect. That's why I must have those coins."

I heard light footsteps in the attic. Dorothy must be back, I thought to myself. "I'm not sure what coins you're looking for, but if you tell me what you know, maybe I can help." He seemed to believe me.

"Before my Dad died he told me Dorothy had sent him a letter. The letter that stated there were Spanish coins hidden by Dorothy's husband that belonged to him."

"Did your Dad tell you where the coins were hidden?"

"My Dad was very ill at the time and was taking medicine to control his pain. He just said something about one of Dorothy's paintings would show me where the coins were located. After Dad died I collected all of Dorothy's paintings from the house. None of them provided a clue to the whereabouts of the coins. I sold the paintings to an art collector in New York. He only gave me a thousand dollars for all five of her paintings, though. That was not enough to pay off my debt. Dad died before I could ask him any more questions about the coins. Since you were so interested in Dorothy's painting at the auction you must know about the coins."

I heard the faint footsteps in the attic again. Was Dorothy trying to tell me something? "Walter, I don't know where the coins are hidden, but maybe they are in the attic. Have you tried looking for them there?"

Walter was quickly losing what little patience he had. He stood and pointed the gun at me. "Show me how to get to the attic."

"Okay, stay calm. The stairs are at the end of the hall, this way." I held my hands above my head as he followed closely behind me with the gun pointed at my back. "You just pull this cord and the stairs will retract."

With Walter's one good hand occupied he directed me, "Pull the stairs down."

I pulled on the cord and the stairs unfolded in front of me. I looked up into the attic opening and there was no sign of Dorothy's ghost. I started praying underneath my breath. Please be there Dorothy. I need your help.

Walter jabbed me in the back with the gun. "You climb up first and I will follow. Don't try anything or I will shoot."

I slowly started walking up the stairs. When I reached the top I looked toward the window where the easel sat and gasped. Dorothy was standing there, but not as I had previously seen her. She looked just like she did when she was alive.   She was wearing a pretty cotton flowered dress, her wavy, gray hair rested on her shoulders. Dorothy put her figures to her lips to signal me to be quiet.

"I'm coming up. Don't try anything funny. Wait at the top of the stairs so I can keep an eye on you."

Since Walter only had one hand, he had to place the gun in the waist of his jeans and use his one good hand to assist him in climbing the ladder. I looked back toward the easel and Dorothy was gone. Suddenly she reappeared right next to me. When Walter poked his head into the attic opening Dorothy jumped in front of me. As Walter lifted his leg to take the last step he looked up.

"It can't be. You're dead!"

Startled by the sight of Dorothy, he lost his grip and fell off the ladder onto the floor below. The impact caused Walter's gun to become dislodged from the waistband of his jeans. The gun landed out of Walter's reach. I raced down the steps and grabbed the gun as Walter moaned from his injuries.

"Don't move, or I'll shoot!" I yelled as I pointed the gun at Walter. He knew his plan had failed.

"I killed Dorothy. There is no way she survived. I saw her death notice in the paper," Walter mumbled to himself.

"You killed Dorothy?" I tried to wrap my brain around what Walter had just confessed. "Why did you kill her?"

"I was afraid my Dad was going to marry her. My Dad had been battling cancer on and off for several years. If he married Dorothy, she would get everything he owned. I would get nothing after he died. I just couldn't let that happen."

I couldn't believe my ears. I started to shake, I was so angry. I realized I could easily kill this man without any regret. He was truly evil. I took a couple of deep breaths trying to control my emotion. Then I remembered being woken each morning at 3AM and asked, "What time did you kill her?"

Walter was confused by my question and hesitated, "What?"

"You heard me," I poked him in the leg with the gun. "What time did you kill Dorothy?"

"I don't know. I think it was around 3AM."

I realized that that was what Dorothy had been trying to tell me by waking me at 3 AM. Then I heard Harper walk through the front door. With a sudden sense of relief I yelled, "Harper, I'm back here!"

Harper took one look at the situation and took control. "Give me the gun."

Shaking badly, I handed the gun to Harper. I was starting to get hysterical. "Walter killed Dorothy," I kept repeating.

"I need you to call the police while I keep an eye on Walter. Can you go to the kitchen and dial 9-1-1?" Harper calmly asked me.

I nodded my head yes as I held back a sob. After dialing the police, I remembered Max. What did Walter do to Max? I hurried back to the hall where Harper was still holding Walter at gunpoint as he lay on the floor. "What did you do with Max?"

Walter just smiled and didn't say a word. "You bastard!" I yelled as I reached down and grabbed Walter's injured arm. "Unless you want me to remove this bandage so you can bleed to death, tell me what you did with Max."

"Okay, okay calm down and let go of my arm," Walter screamed from pain. "He is sleeping soundly in the pantry."

I opened the pantry door and Max was lying on the floor. I watched as his chest rose up and down as he breathed deeply. He was alive. I gently shook Max and called out his name. Max groggily opened his eyes. "It's okay, boy, I'm here." With all my strength, I lifted my sixty pound golden retriever and laid him softly on the sofa.

"What did you give him?" I yelled at Walter.

"I would answer her if you know what is best for you," Harper said.

"I gave him a hot dog with sleeping pills inside it. It's a trick I learned burglarizing homes."

I couldn't believe how heartless and cruel this man was. The police finally arrived. They called an ambulance to take Walter to the hospital to make sure he didn't break anything when he fell down the stairs and to examine his arm with the missing hand. I explained to the officer about Walter looking for some money and hoping to find some in the attic before he fell. I left out the fact that Dorothy's ghost was the one that caused Walter to fall down the stairs. I informed the officer that Walter confessed to murdering

Dorothy. The officers seemed to be as surprised as me when I shared that information.

By the time the police cleared out of my house, Max was waking up and returning to his normal self. He jumped off the sofa and shook from head to tail. Still a little wobbly, I hugged and supported him. "I was so scared I had lost you! You're such a good boy!" I rubbed him all over and gave him a big hug. The realization of what had just happened sank in. I started to cry uncontrollably. Harper held onto me. He comforted me until I was all cried out and felt better.

"I am so sorry for falling to pieces. I don't know what came over me. The last few days have been so crazy."

"You have been through a lot lately and have stayed strong through it all. I just think you reached your tipping point. When I walked in the house and saw you holding a gun pointed at the man on the floor I was so afraid he had hurt you."

"No, he didn't get a chance to hurt me. In fact, you will never guess who saved me."

"You told the police Walter was looking for money. You coaxed him upstairs where he lost his footing and fell down the stairs. That gave you the opportunity to grab the gun. That's not what happened?"

"I thought the police would think I was crazy if I told them the whole story. Dorothy's ghost appeared at the top of the stairs and scared Walter. That's why he fell down the stairs and why he confessed to killing her."

"Seriously?"

"Yes. Maybe she can rest in peace now that her murderer has been caught."

"But what made Walter think there would be money in the attic?"

"Well, I didn't exactly tell the police the whole truth about that, either. Walter, Jr. was looking for the Spanish coins that his father told him about before he died. He hadn't seen the letter, but his father told him that one of Dorothy's paintings held the clue to where the coins were hidden. Walter, Jr. thought I knew where the coins were. When I heard a noise in the attic I hoped that Dorothy was trying to tell me something. That's why I persuaded Walter to go up in the attic to find the coins."

"You're making my head hurt."

I gently kissed Harper's temple. "Thanks for showing up just at the right time to rescue me once again. I had planned to fix you a nice supper so we could relax and enjoy the evening together, before all this happened."

"How about we go to the Drive-in Diner for some hamburgers and milkshakes? That way Max can come with us and we can buy him a deluxe hamburger to devour as a reward for being so brave."

"That sounds perfect! I am suddenly starved after today's adventure."

# Nine

Tuesday morning I woke to the sound of the phone at daybreak. I looked at the caller ID, it was my mother. "Unbelievable," I said under my breath. "Hi, Mom. Do you have any idea what time it is?"

"Your Dad just opened the paper and on the front page the headline reads *Dorothy Evanston's Murderer Caught*. The article said you were held at gunpoint last night. That you were able to grab the gun and hold the murderer until police arrived. Young lady, you have some explaining to do. Are you trying to give me a heart attack?"

I held the receiver away from my ear so as not to damage my eardrum. "Calm down, Mom. I can explain everything." I proceeded to tell her the story, but left out the fact of the hidden coins and Dorothy's ghost. I just simply indicated that Walter was in desperate need of funds and thought I could provide him with some. Thirty minutes later my mom was satisfied that I was no longer in danger. She was glad to hear that Harper had arrived just in time to save me. My Mom was now indebted to Harper for saving her little girl. She would be forever grateful to him. He no longer had to worry whether my parents approved of him or not, for he now walked on water in their eyes. I hung up the phone and kissed Harper playfully. "Have I told you how much I love you lately?"

"No, I think you should tell me again," he joked. Harper held me by the shoulders and kissed me passionately. "Oh my gosh, look what time it is! You're going to be late for work." Unfortunately, my Mom's impromptu phone call took longer than I thought.

Harper kissed me quickly one more time. "I plan to pick up where we left off this evening." He gave me a wicked smile as he hurriedly dressed.

I went to the kitchen and placed a pop tart in the toaster. Then I took Max for a quick pee. As I walked back in the house Harper was rushing out with the pot tart in his mouth.

"I'll call you once I get to work," he mumbled with his mouth full.

As Harper closed the door, I rushed to shower and dress for work. The fourth of July celebration was only four days away. I needed to get to the store to prepare for what I hoped would be a good week of sales. The town bustled with activity in preparation for the big celebration. Vendors were putting up their tents along the river to sell food and crafts. The amusement rides were also being assembled for a day of fun for the kids.

The news of my near demise was all over town. The phone hardly stopped ringing all day at the shop as friends and patrons checked to make sure that I was all right. Thank goodness Gloria was helping me or I never would have been able to keep up with the customers. By the end of the day I was exhausted. The last customer finally left and I took a seat to give my ankle a rest.

Gloria asked, "How are you holding up? I know last night must have been traumatic for you."

"I'm okay. Luckily today we were so busy I didn't have much time to dwell on what happened. With Walter behind bars I should have nothing to worry about now."

"What about the Spanish coins? Are you any closer to locating them?"

"Walter, Sr. may have been the only person who understood the clue in Dorothy's letter to him. Without Dorothy's painting there maybe no way to decipher the letter and where her husband hid the coins."

"Who knows? Dorothy's ghost may come back to help you find the coins," Gloria laughed.

"I hope she can now rest in peace with her murderer in jail. It has been a long day. Why don't you head home while I lock up? Thanks for you help today. I couldn't have handled all the customers without you."

"Always glad to help. I'll see you in the morning!" Gloria yelled as she walked out the door.

"All right Max, are you ready to go home and get something to eat?" Max responded by jumping up from his comfortable spot and barking happily.

I arrived home and cautiously opened the front door. I hesitated and listened to make sure the house was empty and there were no more intruders. I looked around each room to make sure everything was as I had left it this morning. All seemed in place and I breathed a sigh of relief. Harper was due around 7:30 for supper. That gave me an hour to soak in a hot bath and heal my aches and pains from the last few days.

I filled the tub with water and poured in some scented bath oil. I removed the soft cast from my injured ankle and slipped into the heavenly warm water. "Oh, this feels wonderful!" I said out loud. I closed my eyes and rested my head on a towel against the lip of the tub. Images of last night raced through my head. Walter with the gruesome bloody bandage around his arm where his hand used to be, the sight of the gun in his other hand, and the lovely appearance of Dorothy's ghost looking so alive. Then I must have drifted off to sleep.

Harper's voice woke me from my trance. "Maggie, where are you!"

The tub water had cooled. "Crap! I must have fallen asleep. I'm in the bathroom!   I'll be right out!" I yelled back at Harper. I hurriedly dried my pruned body then slipped on a soft cotton Gator football team shorts and jersey. So much for making a special supper to thank Harper for all he has done for me. I walked out of the bedroom barefoot with my right leg back in my soft cast.

"I am so sorry. I fell asleep and didn't get supper cooked. Today was a zoo at work. The phone wouldn't stop ringing with people asking me about last night. The gossip hot line was definitely running in overdrive."

Before I could continue, Harper's muscular arms wrapped around my neck and he kissed me on top of my head.

"I couldn't stop thinking about you today at work. I couldn't get last night out of my mind and had trouble concentrating. God was definitely watching over us. Things could have turned out so much worse."

I interrupted, "God and Dorothy were watching out for us."

"Okay, I will give Dorothy some credit too. It made me realize how close we have grown in such a short time."

Still wrapped in Harper's arms, I told him, "I feel the same way. You have become such a significant part of my life and soul. You seem to know what I am thinking before I speak," I laughed.

"I bought you something on the way home from work today."

"You did? I love surprises! What did you get me?" I asked like an eager child.

To my surprise Harper got down on one knee in front of me. "I was going to wait until the fireworks on the fourth of July, but after seeing you tonight I don't want to spend another minute apart. Maggie, I want to spend every waking minute with you. I want us to make lasting memories together until the day we die. I want to protect you and provide for you. You would make me the happiest man in the world if you would marry me." Harper opened the box he pulled from his pocket. There was a beautiful diamond ring.

Tears ran down my face as I looked into Harper's eyes. "Yes, of course I will marry you!"

Harper stood up and lifted me off the ground and swirled me around. He kissed me passionately then placed the diamond on my finger. I held my hand out in front of me to admire the addition to my ring finger. "Not too shabby for someone that just

87

graduated from college. This must have cost you a fortune. You shouldn't have spent so much, but I'm happy you did." I kissed Harper again to show my appreciation.

"Don't worry. I have a good job now and can afford to splurge occasionally. Especially when it comes to you."

"How about we celebrate with a grilled cheese sandwich and a bowl of chicken noodle soup for supper? I think I've got a bottle of wine that will go with that," I joked.

After supper Harper and I finished the wine. I spent the evening snuggled in Harper's embrace, feeling so happy and safe.

The next morning Harper and I agreed we should share the news of our engagement together with our families. After work Harper planned to meet me at home and then we would drive to my parents first and then to his sister, Sylvia's. I placed the engagement ring in my dresser for safe keeping so no one at work would see it. The hard part was keeping it from Gloria. It's just about impossible to hide anything from her. Sometimes I think she is psychic, she can read me so well.

Max and I arrived at the store and I started restocking the shelves after being so busy the previous day. It wasn't long before Gloria arrived.

"Good morning, Maggie. Have you recovered from yesterday yet?"

I tried to avoid eye contact with Gloria. "Oh yes. I slept like a rock last night."

"I bet you did."

"What is that supposed to mean?"

"You know. I'm sure Harper is why you're glowing today," she laughed.

"You're horrible," I blushed as I remembered our love making.

"When is he going to put a ring on that finger and make you an honest women in God's eyes?"

I hesitated and couldn't come up with a quick response.

"Maggie, are you hiding something from me?"

"Gloria, if I tell you something you have to promise not to tell anyone until tomorrow."

"Of course, dear. You know you can trust me with your secret."

"Harper asked me to marry him last night." I smiled innocently. "We want to tell our families in person tonight, so you can't say a word. If my Mom finds out before Harper and I have a chance to tell her together she will disown me."

"Oh Maggie! I am so happy for you. You have my word. My lips are sealed."

Customers picked up as the day progressed and before I knew it the day was gone. Gloria said good night and I hurriedly closed out the register so I could meet Harper. Before I could lock the door, I heard the bell ring. I looked up. "I'm sorry, we're closed."

A large man stood in the entrance of the store. I immediately knew this man was no customer. I moved slowly to where I hide a gun under the counter near the register, while I tried to smile at the man and politely asked, "Can I help you?"

"Don't move another inch or I will put a bullet in your head."

Max started to growl. "You'd better do something with that mutt or he is dead."

"Don't shoot him!" I begged. "He won't hurt you. I'll place him in the back room." I grabbed Max by the collar. "Come on, boy. It's all right. You stay back here for a little while," I calmly told Max. I would die if anything happened to Max.

"Open the register and give me the cash. No funny business or I will shoot." I had made a bank run at lunch so there was only about five hundred dollars in the register. I opened the drawer and pulled out all the cash. "Here, take it and leave."

He looked at the money. "You must think I am an idiot. I know you have a lot more than this."

"Sales have been slow lately. That's all I have." I tried to convince the robber.

"Walter tells me you have his twenty-thousand dollars he owes me. It's too bad about his hand and all. I know you wouldn't want the same thing to happen to you."

All the color drained from my face. "Walter is wrong. I don't have his money. There is no way I can come up with twenty-thousand dollars."

"We will see about that. Turn around!" he yelled, still pointing the gun at me. He zip tied my wrists together and jerked me toward the door.

I suddenly remembered one of Oprah's shows instructing you that if you ever get kidnapped, never let the kidnapper place you in their car. I had to do something to get-a-way without getting shot.

The gunman walked to the door and looked down the street. The street was empty this time of evening with all the stores closed. "Don't you even think about screaming or you will be sorry." He grabbed my restrained arms and pulled me close to him with the gun stuck in the center of my back. He pushed me out the door toward his car, parked in front of the store. I tried to break free from his grasp and run, but he held my arms so tightly it felt like my bones may crush. He opened his car trunk, shoved me inside, and threw a bag over my head. Before I could break loose the trunk door slammed shut, engulfing me in darkness. I heard the engine start. I kicked the lid of the trunk hoping someone would hear me. I felt around the trunk for something I could use as a weapon. After driving a very short distance the car suddenly came to a stop. Oh God, help me figure a way to get out of this mess. The trunk opened and I was lifted out and quickly shoved up the steps into a building. I fell to the floor. The bag was removed from my head. The room was dimly lit and I noticed the windows of the building had been boarded up. The air inside was stale, humid, and it was about one hundred degrees.

"What do you want from me? I told you I don't have that kind of money."

"Shut up! You say you don't have the money. You will call someone then who can get it for you. If I don't have my money by tomorrow evening you're dead." He shoved a cell phone in my face. "What number do you want me to dial?"

# Ten

I knew Harper should be at my house by now, wondering where I was. I gave the kidnapper his cell phone number and waited for Harper to answer. After two short rings I heard Harper's voice.

"Harper, it's Maggie."

"Are you all right? I was just about to go search for you."

"Listen to me very carefully. A friend of Walter's came to collect the twenty-thousand dollars Walter owes him. I want you to call my Dad and get the money from him. Don't let my Mom know what is going on. Get Max out of the storage room at my shop."

Before I could say another word the phone was jerked out of my hand. The kidnapper spoke to Harper. "I will meet you at the top of the Memorial bridge tomorrow night at nine. I'll be wearing a red baseball cap. If I see any signs of police or a set up, Maggie is dead. Place the money in a green backpack. Once I receive the money I will tell you where Maggie can be found." The line went dead.

\*\*\*

Harper couldn't believe what he had just heard. Someone had kidnapped Maggie. He immediately called Maggie's parents' house hoping to speak to her dad. "Hello Mrs. Thompson, this is Harper, Maggie's boyfriend. Is Mr. Thompson home? I wanted to see if he was available to go fishing tomorrow." He tried to speak calmly even though inside his adrenaline was soaring. He didn't want Mrs. Thompson to suspect something was wrong.

"Oh, he will always make time to go fishing. He's working on a friend's boat right now. Can I have him call you when he returns home?"

"Does he by any chance have a cell phone where I can reach him?"

"He does, but you know how bad the signal can be around here. He may not be in range. You know, Maggie and you should plan to come to supper on Sunday. We would love to get to know you better."

"That's very nice of you. I'll talk to Maggie about it when I see her. I'm sure she would love for us to come. Could I have Mr. Thompson's cell phone number?" Harper reminded her before she changed the subject again.

Finally, Harper had Mr. Thompson's cell phone number. He quickly ended the conversation with Maggie's Mom. "I've got to run, Mrs. Thompson. See you on Sunday." Then he hung up before she could say another word.

Harper dialed the cell phone number he had been given. It rang several times and he was afraid it might go to voicemail.

"Hello."

"Mr. Thompson?"

"Yes."

"This is Harper, Maggie's boyfriend."

"Is Maggie all right?"

"That's why I'm calling you. She needs your help." Harper explained what little he knew of Maggie's predicament. Once finished, there was silence at the other end of the line. Harper was afraid the call may have dropped off.

Maggie's Dad tried to control the anger that was building inside of him. He finally said, "I will get the money. Can you meet me in an hour at my boat repair business?"

"Yes, Maggie showed me where it's located. I'll see you shortly."

"Don't worry son, we'll get Maggie back."

Harper felt a little better knowing he didn't have to carry the burden of rescuing Maggie on his own. He knew Mr. Thompson wouldn't let anyone hurt his little girl.

Before heading to Mr. Thompson's boat repair business, Harper needed to find Max. He pulled up to the front of Maggie's shop and found the door unlocked. He called, "Max!" Max barked wildly and Harper found him behind the door in the back room. Max leaped out as soon as he opened the door and jumped on him, almost knocking him over with the force. He kneeled down to Max's level and was greeted by one ecstatic dog who proceeded to lick his face profusely. Harper dried his face with his sleeve and tried to reassure Max that everything was all right. He loaded Max into his truck and let him ride shotgun in the front seat. He stopped by Maggie's house just long enough to feed Max. He didn't have the heart to leave Max behind after what he had been through, so Max eagerly joined Harper in the truck. Max, still recovering from his scare tried to sprawl across Harper's lap as he quickly drove to the boat repair business to meet Maggie's Dad.

Harper pulled into the gravel parking lot.  He immediately noticed all the cars. "What's going on?" Harper feared Maggie's Dad had told the police about Maggie being kidnapped. He got out of the truck and waited for Max to jump down to the ground beside him. He cautiously walked inside the office area. The room was packed with men all talking at once.

"Harper, I'm glad you're here." The room became quiet. "These men are going to help us get Maggie back safely."

"The kidnaper made it perfectly clear, if I contact the police or in any way set up a trap, he will kill Maggie."

"Not to worry. These men are not police. They are all my fishing and hunting buddies that I trust with my family's life. They won't share our plan with anyone and will do whatever it takes to bring Maggie home safely. They will blend into the crowd on the bridge tomorrow night to watch the fireworks. They will place themselves strategically so as to cover every angle. Once the kidnapper makes his move and approaches you to retrieve the money they will move in to block his path. They will protect you and make sure the guy does not run off with my money without telling you where Maggie is located first."

Harper looked around the room. The men ranged in age from forty to seventy. Some had large beer guts. Most were dressed in some sort of camouflage attire. You could tell they were all outdoors men and knew how to handle a weapon. Maggie's Dad was right. They would blend in nicely with the townspeople that will be by the waters edge waiting for the fireworks to begin tomorrow night. "All right, so what is your plan?"

"Well, you go to the bridge as instructed. I will place twenty-thousand dollars in cash in a green backpack as instructed, and deliver it to you tomorrow afternoon. Make sure you arrive at the bridge early enough to beat the crowd trying to find a good spot to view the fireworks. Station yourself at the top so you will have a good view in all directions. When the kidnapper approaches you, make sure he provides you with the location as to where Maggie can be found before you hand him the money. Once you hand over the backpack, that will be our sign that the deal is complete and we will take him out when he tries to leave."

"You know he will have a gun. What if he starts shooting?"

"Police presence will be high during the event, so I don't think he will do anything stupid. But just in case, we will have a few weapons of our own."

At this point the less I knew about their weapons was probably the better, Harper thought.

"Return here tomorrow at five. I will give you the money and go over everything one last time to make sure everyone understands their role."

Harper drove to Sylvia's with Maggie on his mind. It was now nine at night. He could only imagine what Maggie was going through. On the way he devised a story to tell his sister so she wouldn't be suspicious that something was wrong.

As soon as he walked in the door with Max, Harper was greeted by Sylvia. "Well, I am surprised to see you! Why aren't you staying with Maggie tonight, and who do we have here?" Sylvia reached down to pat Max.

95

Harper hated deceiving his sister, but the whole town would know what was going on if he told her. "Maggie had to go out of town unexpectedly and asked me to watch Max for her tonight. I hope you don't mind?"

"Of course not. I miss having a dog in the house. After Weston, our English setter passed away, I wanted to get another dog, but John wouldn't hear of it. Losing Weston really affected him. I don't think he could bear losing another dog in his lifetime."

"I'm beat. Max and I are going to retreat to the bedroom."

"Are you feeling all right? It's awful early for you to go to bed."

He just wanted to get-a-way from Sylvia's probing questions. "Yes, I'm fine. I just haven't been getting a lot of sleep and I'm tired. I will see you in the morning."

Since tomorrow was the fourth of July, Maggie's store was scheduled to be closed. Harper didn't need to come up with a story to tell Gloria. He was also off work tomorrow for the holiday. Harper climbed into bed but sleep would not come. He could only imagine what Maggie must be going through and it ate him alive. He felt so helpless that he could not do anything to save her until tomorrow. Max sensed something was wrong and laid his enormous head across Harper's chest. He gently stroked Max's head to calm him down and let him know he was safe. He finally drifted off to sleep late into the night with the only sound in the room coming from Max as he snored away.

# Eleven

After talking briefly with Harper, the kidnapper shoved me into a dark storage room. It was so stifling hot I could barely breathe. "Please don't lock me in here," I begged. "I will die from heat exhaustion."

"This is to make sure you behave while I am gone." He shoved a gag in my mouth as I struggled to stop him.

The door was slammed shut and I was engulfed in darkness. I sank to the floor in total despair. My hands were still tied behind my back. Sweat was dripping down my face into my eyes burning them. I blinked several times trying to adjust to the darkness. There were boxes stacked along the wall a few feet away. I managed to stand back up using the wall as leverage. I searched through the boxes to see if I could find something I could use to cut my hands free. I lifted the flap of one of the boxes and was disappointed at what I found. It was full of books. I looked closer to read the title of one of the books in the darkness. It read, "Holy Bible." The box was full of bibles. I felt that was a sign from God. He was with me and would help protect me. I listened and could hear traffic. I must be close to a road. It suddenly dawned on me, the kidnapper must have placed me in the old abandoned church on Main Street. I was on the edge of town. I've got to find a way to escape, I thought to myself. I walked to the door and turned around to grasp the door knob with my restrained hands. I twisted with all my might, hoping it would turn, but it wouldn't budge. With my mouth gagged the exertion caused me to gasp for air. It felt like I was trying to breathe through water, the air was so heavy. I started to feel light-headed and feared I may pass out. I sank back down to the floor and concentrated on slowing my breathing. Everything faded to darkness.

The next thing I knew, the gag was being removed from my mouth. I blinked several times trying to focus. There was a hand holding a bottle of water up to my lips for me to drink. I greedily drank the water being offered to me. I looked up to see who the hand belonged to. It was a woman. She appeared much older than she probably was. Her hair was jet black with streaks of red. I was drawn to her dark eyes which were covered in blue eye shadow and deep blue eye liner. Her lips were painted with bright red lipstick. Under all the make-up there were bruises she attempted to hide. It was difficult to tell her age for she tried to dress older than she appeared. She couldn't be more than eighteen years old. She was tall, at least six inches taller than me and wore heels making her appear even taller. She was skinny and wore tight fitting clothes to emphasize her curves.

"Can you stand? I was told to take you to the bathroom," the woman spoke softly.

"Can you help me up? I don't think I have the strength to get up on my own. I am a bit light-headed from the heat." I wanted her to think I was weak and no way a threat, which was not far from the truth.

She reached down and supported me as I pulled myself up. After regaining my balance she helped me out of the dark closet. It must be morning for I could see the bright sunlight through the slats in the wood over the windows. I squinted from the light until my eyes had a chance to adjust. "Can you remove the restraints from my hands?"

"I don't think that's wise. Roy will kill me if you get-a-way."

"Due to heat exhaustion and this boot on my leg, I am hardly a threat. Can you at least tie my hands in the front? That way it will be easier for me to use the bathroom."

She evaluated my state while she decided what to do. "I guess that would be all right," she finally decided.

I had to get this girl to trust me. She cut the zip tie from my wrists. Pain shot through my hands as the blood returned. "Oh, thank you," I said as I rubbed them trying to get the feeling to return. I held my hands out in front of me so she could see I was cooperating. She secured my hands again, this time using a piece of rope she found laying on the floor. She tied my wrists looser so my circulation was not cut off.

The bathroom was just on the other side of the room. She opened the door for me to go inside. I walked in and reached to close the door.

"Sorry, the door stays open."

I was disappointed, but the bathroom had no windows so there was really no way for me to escape. The bathroom didn't appear to have been cleaned in quite some time. I had on the cotton pastel dress that I had worn to work the previous day. I managed to squat over the commode and not touch the seat with my bottom. I pulled up my underwear. I turned on the faucet and watched as brown water filled the basin. I let it run a little while until the color turned more beige. I washed my hands then splashed some of the lukewarm water on my face and neck. The water cleaned the sweat from my eyes and face, cooling me slightly.

"All right, that's enough. I've got to put you back in the closet."

"It's like an oven in there and it's only going to get worse as the heat of the day increases. Can you stay with me a little longer out here in the daylight? I promise I won't try anything."

She hesitated, trying to decide what to do. "Sit on the floor in the middle of the room so I can keep an eye on you. But I can't stay for long."

I followed her instructions and sat on the floor with my legs extended out in front of me. I tried to loosen my soft cast. My leg had swollen from the heat and my ankle was throbbing. The boot felt like it weighed a ton and was saturated with sweat. The floor was dirty, but better than being in the closet. "My name is Maggie, by the way. I own the Treasures and More store on St. Johns Avenue. Maybe you have heard of it? I started the store by collecting items from garage sales. I found this beautiful bracelet

99

last week with purple stones and shells. After Roy releases me you should stop by and check it out. It would go perfect with those earrings you're wearing."

The young girl lifted her hand to her ear to feel her earrings as if trying to remember which pair she was wearing. She looked so sad.

I continued to ramble on in hopes of making a connection with the girl. "Every Friday night after the store closes I teach a quilting class. It gives the women in the community a chance to get together without any men around. We laugh and eat too many desserts while we sew. You should stop by one Friday night. Women of all ages attend."

"I've never tried to sew anything," she shyly responded. She lit a cigarette as I continued talking.

"It's easy. I'm sure you would pick it up fast. It's not as much about sewing as it is having a night out with just women to talk to. We help solve each others problems while we eat and sew."

"I don't think you can help solve my problems." She inhaled and blew out a long puff of cigarette smoke.

"You would be surprised." I told her about the women that attended and their different backgrounds and ages. Lastly, I told her about Joanne. "Joanne is a woman you would love. She struggled with an abusive husband for years, who almost killed her. She managed to escape the relationship and currently works as a department store manager. She started The House of Hope just off of Crill Avenue about a year ago to help women like herself escape from an abusive boyfriend or husband. I noticed the bruise under your eye. Did someone hit you?"

She moved her hand to cover her face. "It was just an accident. I tripped over a step."

"I understand accidents happen, but if you ever need a place to go, Joanne or I can help." I felt like I was making progress when Roy came storming into the room.

100

"What is she doing out here? I told you to give her some water, let her pee, and put her back in the closet. Now do as I told you! Put the gag back around her mouth and lock her back in the room."

She threw her cigarette to the ground and without a word helped me stand. She walked me back to the closet. She placed the gag back around my mouth. She whispered, "Sorry."

I had made a connection. I was engulfed in darkness again. I heard the door being locked, then silence again. My hands were bound loose enough this time that I was able to wiggle out of the ropes tied around my wrists. I removed my gag and start to yell, "Help!" I yelled until I was hoarse and so thirsty I thought I might faint again. The brick walls of the church, along with the traffic noise, drowned out my screams for help. I figured it must be around six o'clock by now. The money exchange should occur in just a few hours. I needed to stay conscious and not pass out from the heat. When the sound of the fireworks exploding begins I need to be prepared to get-a-way. I started to get dizzy and sank back down to the floor. Sweat was dripping down my face. I felt like I was running out of oxygen. I tried to catch my breath but I was getting so sleepy. I closed my eyes and drifted off to an unconscious state.

# Twelve

Harper woke the next morning after only about three hours of sleep with a wet nose pressed against his face. Max was ready to get up. "All right, boy. I'm awake. Give me a second and I will take you out." Harper grabbed some clothes thrown at the bottom of the bed and quickly dressed. His brain slowly woke to the realization of what had happened to Maggie and the looming money exchange. The smell of coffee led his nose to the kitchen.

"Good morning, little brother," Sylvia cheerfully announced. "How did you sleep last night?"

"Okay." He grabbed a mug from the cupboard and poured a cup of coffee.

"You don't sound okay. Will Maggie be back in town today?"

"Yes, she plans to arrive later this evening."

"Are you and Maggie going to watch the fireworks together tonight?"

"Yes, we planned to if she gets back in time." It was not too much of a lie, since they had planned on attending, before she was kidnapped. Max barked loudly, reminding Harper he still needed to go out. This gave Harper a good excuse to get-a-way from his sister before she could ask any more questions.

"Come on Max, let's go for a run." Running always helped clear Harper's head and brought everything back into perspective. This morning he ran in short bursts to allow Max time to mark a few trees on his route. After about an hour of sweating he felt better. Upon returning to Sylvia's, he gave Max a bowl of food and jumped in the shower to cool off. He let the water run over his head for a long time as his thoughts turned to Maggie. He knew she was not getting to enjoy the pleasures of a cool shower this morning. He almost felt guilty for having the luxury. She was probably hungry and feeling very alone. It tortured him thinking about how frightened she must be.

Feeling more alert after his run and shower, Harper gathered up his things he would need for the day. "I'm leaving and won't be home tonight!" he yelled to Sylvia as he walked out the door with Max in tow. He didn't want to give his sister a chance to ask any more questions. He just hoped that he would be safely with Maggie tonight and this nightmare would be over.

Harper arrived at Mr. Thompson's boat repair business early, hoping to go over plans once again for that night. He walked in and Max happily greeted Mr. Thompson. He was sitting behind his work bench and looked up as Harper walked in. His red puffy eyes indicated he also didn't get much sleep.

"Good morning, sir."

"You can stop with the sir stuff. All my friends call me Skip, short for Skipper. I sneaked out of the house early this morning before my wife could start asking me questions. I was just going to get some breakfast. Have you had anything to eat this morning?"

"No, I don't have much of an appetite."

"I understand, but you need to eat something so you will be in good shape tonight to deal with whatever comes your way."

Max and Harper rode with Skip in his truck to a local restaurant on the river. The meals are served outside on a covered deck so Max could join them. They found a table in the shade and Harper instructed Max to lie down. After their morning run Max was exhausted and obeyed the command without hesitation. He curled up by Harper's feet.

They placed their order and Skip reminisced about Maggie. "My wife and I tried to have children for many years. We had just about given up when she became pregnant with Maggie. I of course wanted a boy, but was thrilled when Maggie was born. She never made me regret for a second she wasn't a boy. She was not a fussy baby and rarely cried. Even when she fell down and hurt herself she didn't whine. She was always so brave. As she grew older she was so inquisitive and we enjoyed spending time together as I taught her how to hunt and fish at the displeasure of her mother. She didn't really care for dolls and dress up like other little girls. She enjoyed getting dirty and being outside. I taught my little girl how to take care of herself and everything she needed to know to survive in this world."

Harper noticed tears starting to well in Skip's eyes as he talked about his daughter. His heart was being torn apart just like his.

Skip paused for a second to recompose himself. "Maggie will fight with whatever strength she has left to stay alive. I doubt whoever has her has any plans of keeping her alive once he has the money. Once you make the exchange tonight and if this guy does not readily hand over Maggie, he is going to be sorry he ever lived. I will do whatever it takes to make him tell us where Maggie is located."

This was a side of Maggie's father Harper hadn't seen before, rage. He was prepared to die if it meant getting his daughter back safely. "Don't worry. I've been up most of the night running through every possible scenario that could occur at the money exchange tonight. I am figuring he will arrive armed, which may leave me at a disadvantage. If he arrives after the fireworks have begun, no one will hear a gunshot and just think it is part of the show. I was thinking I've a better chance of staying alive and getting Maggie back if I don't have all the money with me. I need to coax him someplace where we have the advantage. I will carry just half of the money and tell the kidnapper if he wants the rest he has to show me where Maggie is being held. If by some chance he has Maggie with him, you can be standing by with the rest of the money for the exchange."

"What if he has already killed Maggie and plans to kill you after the exchange?"

"If he tries to shoot me after the exchange and has no intention of telling me where Maggie is located, he is going to have a fight on his hand. But, if he has not killed Maggie and is greedy like I think he is, he will want the rest of the money. Once he takes me to where he is holding Maggie, I will use my cell phone to call you. I will let the kidnapper decide where to have the remainder of the money delivered. Now comes the tricky part. Once the other half of the money is in his possession, there is nothing stopping him from killing both of us."

"Don't worry. I will have your back and my friends will be standing by in case we need them. If he takes you to where he is holding Maggie there will be someone following you."

"Just make sure your friends don't spook the kidnapper before I know where Maggie is being held."

"Understood. It sounds like you have thought through every possibility. I will brief the guys this afternoon. If all goes well this should be over in a few hours. Maggie's Mom is starting to suspect something is up. She keeps calling my cell phone checking to see where I am and what time I will be home. I've got to keep her distracted tonight so she and Grandma don't interfere with our plan. Meet me back at the shop at five. I will give you half of the money in the green backpack and place the other half in a duffel bag."

They had both finished eating what little they could get down of their breakfast. With the events of the day on their mind, neither of them ate much. Harper took Max to the park to play while he tried not to worry. The day was sunny and warm. The park was full of families picnicking with their children, enjoying the day off from work. He smiled as he watched one family flying a kite with their two children, a girl and a boy. He hoped that would be him one day with Maggie.

Harper avoided going back to his sister's house until just about the time to leave to meet Skip with the money. He didn't want his sister to suspect anything was wrong. Harper drove up and quickly walked into the utility room to fill Max's bowl with food.

"Is that you Harper?"

"Yes, I was just feeding Max and then going to put him in my bedroom for the evening. Max is scared of loud noises. He will feel much safer in the confined space of my bedroom."

"Do you want some supper before you leave?"

"No, I'm meeting some friends and then going to town to find a good place to watch the fireworks."

"Good. Maybe I will see you there. I managed to persuade John to take me this year, amazingly enough. You know how much he hates doing anything where there is a large crowd. With the skies forecasted to be clear, the fireworks should be beautiful."

Harper hoped he could avoid running into Sylvia tonight. The last thing he needed was her messing up his plans. He quickly left and drove to the boat repair business to meet Skip. He walked into the office and found himself surrounded by Skip's friends.

"Here is the backpack with half of the money like we discussed." A concerned look crossed Skip's face. "Son, if things start to go wrong, reach for your ear and we will move in."

Harper nodded to acknowledge that he understood. "Hopefully the next time I talk to you will be on your cell phone telling you that Maggie is safe and where to leave the remainder of the money." With no more to be said Harper left with the backpack draped over his shoulder.

He drove to town and found an empty parking space at the base of the Memorial bridge and pulled into it. As soon as he stepped out of the truck he heard Mrs. Thompson calling his name.

"Harper, over here!"

"Crap," he said under his breath. He looked in the direction where his name was being called from and waved at Mrs. Thompson. She motioned for him to come over to where she was sitting with Maggie's Grandmother in lawn chairs, waiting for the show. He didn't want to be rude so he walked over to them.

"Is Maggie with you tonight? I called her house and cell phone several times leaving messages. She hasn't returned any of my calls."

Maggie's Dad shook his head in the background to tell him he was sorry for the confrontation. "She's meeting me later. I'll make sure she returns your phone call when I see her."

"Maggie loves watching the fireworks. It's a good time for two lovers to cuddle, if you know what I mean," Grandma said as she winked at him.

"I've got to run." He quickly retreated before he ran into anyone else he knew. The bridge was already packed with people trying to find the best spot to view the fireworks. He made his way to the top of the bridge, holding the backpack securely under his arm. He looked around for anyone in a red baseball cap. None were in sight yet. The sun was starting to set so it wouldn't be long before the fireworks began. He leaned against the bridge railing as he watched for anyone approaching with a red cap. He recognized several of the men he had seen at Skip's boat repair business. They were nonchalantly mixed in with the crowd along the bridge. He felt a little better just knowing they were close in case the exchange turned bad.

The fireworks started and still no guy in a red baseball cap approached. He started to worry that the kidnapper suspected a trap and backed out. Then he saw a large guy wearing a red cap walking toward him. He took a deep breath. "God help me not to screw this up," he whispered to himself.

"You Harper?"

"Yes."

"Is all the money in the backpack?"

"First, tell me where Maggie is located."

"That's not how this game is going to be played. You give me the money and when I am safely away I will call your cell to let you know where Maggie is being held."

"How do I know you haven't already killed her?"

"I guess you will have to trust me."

107

"Well, I don't trust you which is why there is only half of the money in the backpack. When you show me where Maggie is being held you will received the other half." Suddenly Harper felt a gun pressed up against his ribs.

The guy leaned toward his face and whispered, "That was not the plan. Now you die."

Harper reached for his ear as the sound of gunfire erupted.

# Thirteen

I felt myself being shaken awake. I looked up. The young girl had returned.

"You have to get out of here. Roy never planned to let you go. Once he has the money he will kill you. I was not here. Do you understand? If Roy finds out I helped you escape  he will kill me." She turned to leave.

"Wait! Come with me. I can help you."

"No one can help me." She walked out the back door of the church and disappeared.

I staggered to the door and peeked outside. I could hear the loud booms of the fireworks in the distance. The police station was only about a block away. I was afraid to flag down a car for fear of what might happen. I stayed off Main Street and quickly walked behind the businesses to hide so no one would see me. The police station was in view. Just a little further. I stopped beside a tree to hide in case anyone was watching. I cautiously looked around to make sure there was no one in sight before crossing. I rushed as fast as I could, with my booted ankle, across the road in front of the station. I made it across the street without being seen and quickly entered the police station out of breath. The lobby was quiet, with most of the officers out on patrol. I must have looked a fright. A female police officer approached me and asked if I needed help. I nodded my head yes, trying to catch my breath and hold back my tears. I was finally safe.

I proceeded to tell the officer the story of what had happened. "You need to send some officers immediately to the bridge to intercept the money exchange."

"You stay here. There are several officers downtown patrolling the area while everyone is gathered to watch the fireworks."

She radioed the officers, but from what I could hear, it sounded like they were already busy handling a disturbance.

"I need to take you to the hospital to be examined to collect evidence and make sure you're not injured." The woman officer spoke up after ending her transmission.

"Are the officers going to check the bridge for Roy?"

"They already have Roy in custody."

"What about Harper? Is he all right?"

"An ambulance has transported him to the hospital. The officer I talked to didn't know how badly he was injured. Your father was also on the scene and will meet you at the hospital."

I started to faint and the officer grabbed me. "We better get you to the hospital."

If something has happened to Harper, I will never forgive myself. I laid in the back of the cruiser unable to sit in an upright position. What little energy I had left was sucked out of me once I heard Harper was injured. The officer rushed me to the emergency room with her blue lights flashing and sirens blaring. We were met at the entrance by a nurse with a wheelchair. Before I could ask about Harper I was rushed inside and greeted by my family. My Dad leaned down and held me tightly. It brought back memories of when I was a little girl. Any time I fell down he would hold me tightly, tell me I was fine, and there was no need to cry. I was having trouble holding back the tears now, though.

He quietly asked, "Did he hurt you?"

With tears streaming down my face I shook my head no. Wiping the tears from my cheeks I frantically asked, "Where is Harper? Is he okay?"

"He was shot through the side and should be fine. My buddies tackled Roy as he started to shoot Harper. The gun went off as Roy fell to the ground. The gun was knocked from his hand

110

as several men came down hard on him. Roy was restrained until police arrived."

I looked over Dad's shoulder and Mom was standing quietly, something I had never seen, with tears in her eyes. "Mom, I'm sorry. I didn't mean to make you worry about me."

"My baby. It's my job to worry. I will never stop worrying." She leaned down and gave me a hug. "I knew something was wrong when your Dad made himself very scarce without a good explanation and I couldn't reach you."

The nurse interrupted our reunion. "We better get you checked out to make sure you were not injured."

"Can I see Harper first?"

"The doctor is with him just down the hall. He has been frantically asking for you also." The nurse pushed me to where they were working on Harper.

I entered the exam room and saw Sylvia standing by Harper's side. She looked up and smiled.

"I am so happy to see you. Harper has been driving me crazy from worry about you!" Sylvia reached down and gave me a gentle hug.

Harper lifted his head and grimaced in pain. "Did Roy hurt you?"

I stood up from the wheelchair and walked over to Harper. I grasped his hand and looked into his eyes. "I am just bruised and tired. I thought I might have lost you."

"The bullet managed to miss all my organs and went clean through my side. Your Dad and his buddies stopped Roy from hurting me worse. Roy told me he had killed you. When I heard that my heart stopped." Harper squeezed my hand, not wanting to ever let it go.

"I had an angel watching over me." I leaned down and gently kissed Harper on the lips. "We have a wedding to plan," I whispered. Then I remembered Max. "How is Max? Did you find him in my store?"

"Max is fine and probably sleeping soundly at Sylvia's."

Sylvia spoke up, "Max is no trouble at all and I can watch him until you get back on your feet."

"Thanks for all your help." The last two days had taken their toll on me and I was not sure how much longer my legs could support me in an up right position. I started to get dizzy and grabbed hold of Harper's arm for support.

"Are you all right? Sit down before you fall down."

The nurse grabbed hold of me and eased me back down into the wheelchair. "It's time to let the doctors take care of you," the nurse urged.

"I guess the last two days are catching up with me. I will come and find you as soon as the doctors are finished with me."

I was wheeled away and placed in an exam room. The female officer that had brought me to the hospital stayed close by. The nurse checked my vital signs and then asked, "Please remove all your clothes and slip into this."

The nurse handed me a cotton gown with no back. Once undressed the female officer was handed my clothes and they were placed in an evidence bag. My Mom popped her head into my room.

"Is it all right if I stay with you?"

"Of course Mom," I held out my hand and Mom grabbed hold of it. This was one time I didn't mind having Mom close.

The doctor poked around my stomach with his fingers asking, "Does this hurt?"

"No."

Then he shined a light into my eyes, looked at my tongue and listened to me breathe, using a stethoscope. "How does your ankle feel?"

"Tired like the rest of me."

"I think it's probably healed enough to remove the boot since it's filthy and pretty tattered looking."

Two days of sweating and then walking through the dirt to the police station had taken its toll on my soft cast. It looked and smelled like something I had retrieved from the garbage dump.

112

"You have no idea how happy that would make me to have that thing off my leg."

The doctor laugh and eased it off my foot. "You seem to be in good shape based on what you have been through. Your wrists seem to be the most injured. Let's clean them and place some antibiotic ointment on them so they don't get infected. I'm going to have the nurse start an IV to help replenish your fluids. I need you to rest for several days and to drink plenty of fluids. Your body has gone through a trauma. You may think you're ready to resume your normal life, but you need time to absorb what you have been through and heal mentally as well as physically."

My Mom had sat quietly until now. "I will make sure she does not try to do too much too soon and that she is getting plenty of food and rest."

Ointment was smoothed on my wrists and they were wrapped in gauze as the IV bag attached to my arm slowly dripped. Once the IV bag was empty I was allowed to leave. Dad brought me one of his fishing t-shirts and baggy shorts to wear home. All I wanted to do was rejoin Harper to see how he was doing, then go home and take a long cool shower. My body still felt like it was on fire after baking in that oven for two days.

The nurse wheeled me out of the room and I saw Sylvia approaching with Harper in a wheelchair. There was a large bandage around his waist.

Sylvia hinted to my Mom, "Why don't I buy you a cup of coffee?" She wanted to give us a few minutes alone.

Mom took the hint. "I guess I could use a cup. I will be right back, Maggie."

"What did the doctor say?" Harper asked as he gently reached for my hand.

"I just need a few days of rest. How about you?"

"The wound only required about ten stitches. I will be as good as new in no time. I wish I was staying with you tonight, but I am in no condition to take care of you. I can already feel the affect of the pain medicine the doctor gave me. I don't know how much longer I will be able to keep my eyes open."

"Don't worry. My Mom is not going to let me out of her sight for a few days. Call me tomorrow when you wake up and let me know how you're doing. If you're up to it I might be able to escape for a few hours to visit."

"All right you two, it's late. We should be going," Mom said. She returned with Dad by her side.

"I'm going to pull my truck around front to pick you up," Dad said as he turned to leave.

Harper leaned closer and pulled me to him so he could give me a gentle kiss. "Sweet dreams. I will talk to you tomorrow."

I smiled to myself at how lucky I was to have Harper in my life as Mom pushed my wheelchair to Dad's truck.

# Fourteen

I woke the next morning to the phone ringing off the hook. I covered my head with the pillow, but knew I wouldn't get any more sleep. It was like opening day of deer season in my parents' house, with the excitement of what the day could bring on every deer hunter's mind. I am sure all of my Mom's friends had heard about my kidnapping and were calling to console her. As much as I would like to stay in bed all day long I knew I wouldn't be able to rest. I decided I better face the day and peeled back the covers. I had slept in the large t-shirt Dad had given me at the hospital. I slowly sat up in bed and ached all over. I looked at my bandaged wrists and memories of my abduction came flooding back. I was so lucky. It could have been so much worse.

I stayed on the edge of the bed for a while trying to muster up the energy to move. I missed Harper and wished he was beside me holding me safely in his arms. It felt strange to wake up without Max breathing in my face, and made a mental note to pick him up today. I suddenly remembered that Harper had asked me to marry him before my life was turned upside down. I couldn't wait to tell our families about our engagement. I wanted to start my life with Harper as soon as possible. I slowly stood up and tested my legs to make sure they would hold me. I was a little wobbly after my ordeal. I noticed my reflection in the dresser mirror. My hair stood on end where I had fallen asleep with it still wet. The large t-shirt swallowed me whole. I had lost several pounds in the last two days. I am sure Mom will fix that by stuffing me with food until I explode, I laughed to myself. I gently removed the gauze from my wrists to see how bad they looked. They were red and bruised, but they would heal in a few days. I searched through my old dresser for something to wear. I found a pair of shorts and cool cotton sleeveless shirt I had previously left. I looked at my feet. The boot that had become part of my right foot was pleasantly missing. I didn't have any shoes. Oh well, I'll go barefoot until I can get to my house. I splashed some water on my face to help bring me back to the living. Thoughts of the dirty water I had splashed on my face just yesterday suddenly entered my mind. I worried about the girl that had set me free. Hopefully she found somewhere safe to stay. The phone suddenly rang again, which brought me back to the present. I could hear Mom talking loudly to someone who was asking how I was doing. The whole town must know about my abduction by now. I slowly cracked my bedroom door open and braced myself for my mother's onset of affection. She was definitely a morning person who started her day off full steam ahead.

"Maggie, what are you doing up so early? You need to get your rest."

I wanted to ask my Mom, how do you expect anyone to rest in this house with all the noise, but instead I replied, "I was thinking about the shop. I need to go there this morning and open it for Gloria."

"You will do no such thing, young lady. You heard what the doctor said last night. You need to take a few days to rest."

"Oh Mom, I can't sit around here all day or I will go crazy. I need to run by my house and get some clothes and stop by Sylvia's to pick up Max. It's Friday, so my quilting club is meeting after work."

"I think you could cancel the club for one night. I am sure everyone would understand."

"The club is as much for me as it is for them. It will help me keep my mind off of the last couple of days."

"Well, before you go anywhere you're going to eat a large breakfast. You're as skinny as a rail. A large breeze could blow you over."

Before I could reply, Grandma entered the kitchen. "Good to see you up and about this morning, Maggie. You'd better hang onto that boyfriend of yours. He is definitely a keeper."

"Yes, Grandma, I agree. He is definitely special."

"That reminds me. When Harper called to talk to your Dad on Wednesday I invited him to dinner after church on Sunday. Do you think he will feel up to coming?"

"I don't know, Mom. I'll ask him today and let you know."

Dad walked in and gave me a hug. "How are you doing this morning, sweetie?"

"I'm a little sore, but no worse for wear."

"How about after breakfast I run you by your house so you can pick up some clothes?"

Dad is always my savior. "That would be great!" I said just a little too enthusiastically. Dad knew if Mom and I stayed in the house together for an extended period of time it wouldn't be long before we would be at each others throats. He always seemed to know when I needed to get-away.

After a breakfast of pancakes and enough bacon to give me a heart attack, Dad drove me home. Once Dad and I were alone in his truck he asked, "How are you really doing?" He knew it was hard for me to show any weakness.

"I will be fine Dad. I just need to stay busy so the last few days don't take over my life. It would be very easy for me to hide in my room where it's safe and never come out. But you know that returning to my routine is the best thing I can do."

"Parents always want to protect their children from any harm. Believe me letting you return to your life is not easy for your mother or me. We both know how hard it must be for you and wish we could take away the hurt. We are here for you if you need anything."

I leaned over and kissed Dad on the cheek. "I love you Dad." He pulled into my driveway. I looked at the house and thankfully noticed nothing unusual. It seemed like ages ago since I was here last. Dad understood my hesitation and sat quietly until I was ready to go inside.

"I'll wait for you inside to give you a chance to change. Then I can drive you to your shop to pick up your car."

"Thanks Dad. It won't take me long." I hurriedly showered and found something with long sleeves to cover the abrasions on my wrists. I didn't want people feeling sorry for me and staring at my wounds. I looked in the mirror and felt a little unnerved. My face didn't show it but my insides were in a turmoil. I hesitated, knowing how difficult it was going to be for me to walk in the shop today. I took a deep breath and put on a good face for Dad. "All ready," I cheerfully announced. I didn't want Dad to know how hard this was for me.

My car was where I had left it two nights ago. The streets were quiet this morning and Dad parked in front of my store. I unlocked the door to the shop and walked in with Dad by my side. I was accosted by the memories of the night I was abducted. The register drawer still lay open from when I gave my abductor the money. I knew I would never see that money again. The storage room door was ajar from when Harper found Max. Gloria hadn't arrived yet which was good. I needed the time to digest what had happened here and come to grips with my emotions. Dad stayed quiet and walked with me while I slowly made my way around, checking to make sure I was the only one inside.

"Are you sure you're up to this? The doctor said you should give yourself time to heal before diving back into work."

"I need to do this, Dad. If I don't, my fears will consume me."

The bell above the door rang and I jumped at the sudden noise.

"Maggie, what on earth are you doing here? You should be at home in bed," Gloria scolded. "I can take care of the shop today."

"I already tried that with no success," Dad chimed in.

"I'll take it easy today and let Gloria handle most of the customers. Thanks for dropping me off Dad. I will give you and Mom a call tonight when I get home." I knew they would worry until they heard from me.

Dad left and Gloria helped me straighten up the store. She was unusually quiet and didn't ask me about what had happened. She tried to cheer me up by telling me how much fun she had celebrating the fourth of July. She had attended a big crab boil with all the fixins along with homemade ice cream. It sounded heavenly.

The phone rang and I answered it while Gloria helped a customer. "Harper, I am so glad you called. How are you feeling?"

"I called your parents' house and could not believe it when your Mom told me you were going to work today. Do you think that is such a good idea?"

"You know if I stayed in the same house with Mom for very long I would be pulling my hair out. Now tell me, how are you doing?"

"I'm feeling much better now that the painkiller the doctor gave me has worn off. It gave me crazy nightmares all night long. I'm getting cabin fever and Sylvia is hovering over me like a sick child."

"Do you think I could stop by around lunch and visit with you and pick up Max? I miss having him at the store with me."

"It sounds like you miss Max more than me," he laughed.

"Nonsense, I love you both the same," I joked. "I will see you soon. We have to discuss when we are going to announce our engagement, that is if you haven't changed your mind."

"I didn't know it was possible but the last forty-eight hours have brought me even closer to you. I want to marry you more than ever, and soon!"

A tear came to my eye at the realization that I had almost lost Harper last night. If the bullet had been just a little higher it could have hit his heart instead of his side. I wiped the tear as it ran down my face and recomposed myself. "I love you and will see you in about an hour."

Gloria watched over the store for me while I spent some time with Harper. I snuggled with him in bed and actually fell asleep. I felt so relaxed being with him. I woke up just in time to meet the quilting club.

Gloria must have told everyone in the quilting club to not ask me what had happened. The conversation was normal, talking about their children and what they had gotten into and what crazy thing their husband did this week. That was until a surprise guest arrived. The bell above the door rang and I looked up. It was the girl that had helped me escape from the church. I jumped up from my chair and ran over to hug her.

"I am so glad you came! Let me introduce you to everyone." Then it dawned on me, she never told me her name.

"Hi, I'm Celia."

No one questioned how I knew her or judged her for how she dressed or the color of her hair. She was immediately made to feel part of the group. We all pigged out on brownies and had fun showing Celia how to quilt. As the women started to leave I asked Joanne, "Can you help me with something?"

I motioned for Celia to stay. "Celia, Joanne is the woman I was telling you about that runs House of Hope. Did you want to ask her any questions?".

Joanne knew what I was trying to convey and sat back down at the table so Celia could see she was in no hurry to leave. Celia joined her at the table while I called Harper to tell him I was running a little late. I could tell the conversation between Joanne and Celia was going well when I saw Celia start to cry and Joanne embraced her. After drying their tears Joanne announced, "Celia is going to stay with me for a while."

"I am so pleased to hear that! After what you did for me I was so scared something bad may have happened to you. You deserve so much better in life and I know Joanne will help you find that." I hugged Celia again. "I hope to see you soon. Please stop by any time."

"I had fun tonight. Thanks for trusting me."

Everything that had happened to me in the last few days suddenly seemed clear. God had put me in Celia's path to help her find her way. I drove home with a sense of peace knowing that God was watching over me.

Harper was already inside waiting for me. He didn't want me to be alone. Max followed me inside and jumped on the sofa beside Harper and licked his face with excitement.

"I missed you too, boy." Harper rubbed him all over. They now held a special bond after he had rescued Max.

"Okay Max, give Harper a break. Do you want some food?" At the sound of the word food, Max jumped off the sofa and ran to his food dish.

"There is no doubt that Max missed you. Did you miss me?" I teased.

Harper leaned down and kissed me for a long time to show me how much he missed me, too. I called my parents right away to let them know I was safely home and there was no need to worry because Harper was with me. I changed into some comfortable clothes and plopped on the sofa next to Harper. I no longer felt like I had to try to impress Harper with my appearance. He had seen all sides of me now and that hadn't scared him away.

"Are you hungry? Mom told me she dropped off some food today while I was at work."

"Don't tell Sylvia, but she is not the best cook," Harper laughed.

"Let's see what Mom left us." We peered in the refrigerator at a large beef pot pie, a salad, and an entire chocolate cake.

"I've died and gone to heaven," Harper said.

I microwaved the pot pie and set everything on the table while Harper opened a bottle of wine. We ate like we hadn't eaten in a week. It was so nice to be able to relax with Harper again. We both discussed what had happened while I was being held captive. I hadn't realized how close Harper had come to losing his life. Dad had sugar coated it for me. I was glad to hear that after Roy was shot Dad retrieved the backpack full of his money. I don't know how I would have ever repaid him if he had lost the twenty-thousand dollars. Harper was very upset when I told him where I had been held.

"You were so close. I can't believe no one heard your cries for help."

Then I told him how Celia came to my rescue and about her showing up at the shop tonight. He was happy that I was able to help her after she risked her life to save me.

Harper suddenly changed the subject. "I forgot to tell you, my Mom is coming to town tomorrow. After Sylvia called to let her know I had been shot, she immediately made plans to come down."

"That's great! We can announce our engagement with her present. That reminds me. My Mom wants to know if you're still coming to dinner on Sunday."

"Oh, I forgot when I called looking for your Dad, she invited me. That will be the perfect time to tell your parents about our engagement."

After several hours we were all talked out and I was in desperate need of sleep. We climbed into bed and Harper wrapped his arms tightly around me. Max jumped on the bed and laid his large body across both of us. This was like heaven to me, having both of the men in my life so close. I slept soundly all night with no interruptions.

# Fifteen

After work on Saturday I rushed home to feed Max and to change into something nice. I wanted to look presentable for meeting Harper's Mom. I worried whether she thought I would be good enough for her only son. I had just finished styling my hair with the curling iron when I heard Harper at the door.

"I will be right out!" I yelled. I retrieved my engagement ring from the box hidden in my dresser and slipped it on my ring finger. I held my hand out to admire it. It still hadn't sunk in that Harper and I were getting married. I took one last look at myself in the mirror and decided I could pass inspection. Even though it was in the middle of summer I found a lightweight long sleeved silk blouse to wear with a cotton skirt. I wanted to conceal the red marks on my wrists from the cuts made from the restraints. I hoped Harper's mom wouldn't notice.

"You look gorgeous! You would think it was a special occasion," Harper laughed.

"This is no time to joke. I am a nervous wreck. What if your Mom doesn't like me?"

"Of course she will like you. As soon as she sees how happy you make her son she will love you." Harper leaned down to kiss me.

I placed my hand on his chest to stop him. "You'll mess up my lipstick." I gently kissed him on the lips with a mischievous smile. Then wiped my pink lipstick off his mouth with my fingers.

"We'd better hurry. Sylvia is cooking supper and I don't want to make her wait for us."

Upon arriving, Harper helped me out of his truck and held my quivering hand.

"Stop worrying and just be yourself. My Mom will love you." He pulled my hand to his lips and kissed my fingertips.

I was immediately welcomed by Sylvia upon entering the house. "Supper is ready and Mom is placing all the food on the table. She is anxiously waiting to meet you."

Sylvia led the way to the dining room. She had outdone herself. The table was full of food. "Oh my Sylvia, everything looks delicious."

"Maggie, I would like you to meet our Mom, Helen."

"It's so nice to meet you. Harper has told me many stories about his childhood and what a great mother you are."

"Come here child and let me give you a decent welcoming." She embraced me and squeezed me dearly. "It's so nice to finally meet you. I would say I've heard wonderful things about you, but my son has been keeping you a secret."

"Now Mom, you know I wouldn't hide anything from you," Harper joked. Then he became serious, "If everyone would please take their seats, Maggie and I have something we would like to share with you."

"What is this about? After the scare you gave me this week I hope you have some good news," Helen said with a smile.

Harper held my hand tenderly as he spoke. "Maggie and I have only known each other for a short time, but as soon as I met Maggie I knew I wanted to marry her. I waited to make sure she felt the same way about me before I asked for her hand in marriage. We are engaged!" Harper held out my hand for everyone to see my ring. Sylvia and Helen jumped out of their chairs and hugged us both.

John, Sylvia's husband, shook Harper's hand and told me, "This boy has a good heart and will make you a good husband."

"Congratulations! I am so glad you finally came to your senses and asked Maggie to marry you. I wondered what was taking you so long," Sylvia said.

"I am so happy for you both and look forward to getting to know you better, Maggie." Helen was very proud of her son. I could see tears in her eyes as she kissed Harper on the cheek.

During supper the conversation revolved around the events of the last few weeks.

"How did you two meet?" Helen asked.

"Well, it's kind of a funny story." Harper turned toward me and looked to get my approval before telling the story.

"You can tell them," I said.

"Maggie bumped into me at the hardware store and talked me into helping her install a toilet she didn't need."

I tried to defend myself, "At the time I couldn't think of another way to get Harper to spend the afternoon with me."

We laughed the night away. Helen was going to be in town for the week so I invited her to lunch on Monday. I wanted to show her my home and how much help Harper had been renovating it with me. I also wanted her to visit my shop. We said our good nights and Harper drove me home. He reached for my hand in the car.

"I told you Mom would love you. Thanks for inviting her to lunch on Monday."

"You know I am going to get her to tell me all the embarrassing things you did when you were a little boy."

"I was afraid of that. Just remember, it's my turn tomorrow with your family."

"They already consider you part of the family after everything you have done for me. My Mom is going to be ecstatic when we tell her the news. I hope you didn't plan on a small wedding because my Mom will want to invite everyone in the community."

"Are you sure you just don't want to elope and tell them afterwards?"

"I would love to, but my Mom would disown me. I couldn't do that to her."

The next morning Harper and I attended church together. I hid my engagement ring in my purse so no one would see it. On the way to my parents' house for dinner I slipped it back on my finger. I was still getting used to how it felt on my hand.

Harper laughed. "You will no longer have to hide it after today."

"I will never take it off again." I leaned over and kissed Harper. He pulled into my parents' driveway. Harper held my hand as before to conceal the ring. We walked in and Dad had already made himself comfortable in his recliner. I could hear Mom and Grandma arguing about the lumps in the gravy in the kitchen.

"Why don't you relax with Dad and I will see if I can help in the kitchen?"

The commotion continued as I entered the kitchen. "Is there anything I can do to help?"

"Everything is ready. Why don't you help place the food on the table?" Mom said.

I picked up the serving dishes Mom had filled with food.

"My blazes! What is that on your finger?" Grandma asked.

"Let me see." Mom reached for my hand.

"Harper and I were going to tell you once we got to the table."

"My little girl is getting married!" Mom hugged me and the tears started to flow.

Dad stepped into the kitchen. "What is going on in here? I hope those are tears of joy."

I held my hand out so Dad could see my ring.

Dad turned around and grabbed Harper's hand and firmly shook it. "I couldn't be happier for you both. Welcome to the family, son."

"Stop blubbering you two. The food is getting cold. We'd better eat," Grandma added. Even though Grandma shows a rough exterior I knew she was ecstatic for me.

The meal conversation revolved around wedding questions from Mom. "So have you set a date yet?"

I looked at Harper. "We want to get married as soon as possible." Then I added, "Since we don't have a lot of money we want to keep it simple and small," I emphasized.

"Nonsense, your Dad and I have saved for this day and we want it to be special for you."

I braced myself. Oh Lord, here it comes!

"Of course you will be married in our church which means we need to invite the parishioners. We have to invite your aunts, uncles, and cousins."

"Don't forget I want to invite my friends. I would never hear the end of it if I didn't invite Gertrude," Grandma chimed in.

"We can have the reception at the Charter House on the river," Mom continued. "They have room for a band outside where your guests can enjoy the evening."

I interrupted before she could go any further. "Mom, Harper and I really wanted to keep it intimate and small. Today is July seventh, and if the church is available we would like to get married on July twentieth. What you're planning would take months to organize."

"Don't you worry about a thing. I know you're busy and I can take care of all the details. I can start this afternoon with coming up with the guest list and will start sending out the invitation by Wednesday. I'll get you a menu tomorrow so you can pick the food for the reception. There is a bakery downtown that can make the wedding and groom cakes. All you need to do is find a dress and a tux. How many bridesmaids do you plan on having in the wedding?"

"I haven't really had a chance to think about it," I looked over at Harper in desperation, to get his input.

"Mrs. Thompson, Maggie and I will discuss it later tonight and get back with you tomorrow."

By the time we left my parents I was beyond stressed. What was supposed to be a happy occasion with my family, turned into a circus as always. Mom was still rattling off wedding ideas as we reached the truck. Once inside the safety of Harper's truck, with the doors securely closed, I welcomed the quiet. Harper didn't have much to say on the way home. We arrived home and were accosted by a very excited dog when I opened the door. My mood improved instantly as Max gave me his unconditional love by licking my face as I patted him behind the ears. He barked loudly to let me know how happy he was that I was home, and ready to go for his walk. "I am glad to see you too, boy." I roughed up his fur then rushed to change into some shorts and grabbed his leash. I held out my hand for Harper to join me. With Max leading the way Harper and I walked hand in hand enjoying the warm sunny afternoon along the river.

"I know my Mom can be a bit overwhelming, but she means well. The wedding is not exactly what we had talked about but allowing Mom to do this for us will mean so much to her."

"I understand it's a big deal for her only daughter to be getting married. As long as I don't have to come up with a bunch of groomsmen I'm happy."

I leaned over to kiss Harper. As soon as our lips touched Max took off running. I lost my grip on the leash and Max raced down the street after a cat. "Max, STOP!" My command went unanswered. Max was totally focused on catching up with the cat. Harper and I raced after him. Max turned toward downtown and I lost sight of him. I yelled one more time, "Max, COME!" I was worried he would be hit by a car. Harper and I kept running. We turned at the street corner and stopped, out of breath. Max was sitting in front of the bakery just down the street from my shop. He must have lost sight of the cat and decided to see if he could get a treat from Miss Brenda who works at the bakery. The bakery was closed since it was Sunday, but Max didn't know any better. I walked up to Max and grabbed his leash. "BAD BOY!" I scolded him. "Don't ever do that again. You scared me half to death. What would I do if anything ever happened to you?" Max turned his head and gave me a sad look like he understood what I was saying.

"All right, I think we have had enough exercise for today." We turned to head back home and cut down Third Street. I suddenly stopped and looked at the mural of flowers painted on the side of the building.

"Is something wrong?" Harper asked.

"Remember Dorothy's letter to Walter? She said the painting of the wildflowers by the river held the clue to where the coins could be found."

"Yeah, so?"

"This is the painting she was talking about! It was not a painting she had created, but the mural of Putnam County Wildflowers painted on the side of the building overlooking the river. I think I know where the coins are hidden. Hurry, we need to get home!"

I stopped on the sidewalk leading to my front door. "The passion flowers growing on the trellis are just like the ones in the mural. The next clue was leave no stone unturned." I pointed to the stone edging in front of the flowers. "I bet the coins are buried under one of the stones!"

"Well, there is only one way to find out," Harper said. "Do you have a shovel?"

"Yes, it's in the tool shed out back."

I took Max inside so he wouldn't get in our way and returned to find Harper back outside with a shovel in hand.

"Where should we start?" Harper asked.

"Let's remove the stones in front of the passion flower and see if we find anything."

I helped Harper lift the stones out of the way and piled them in the front yard. "Well, I don't see anything unusual, so I guess we start digging."

Harper carefully pushed the shovel in the ground removing small amounts of dirt with each load. He didn't want to damage whatever maybe buried there. It was not long before the shovel hit something hard. "I think I might have found something!" Harper

129

kneeled down on the ground and removed the rest of the dirt with his hands.

"What is it?" I anxiously asked.

"It appears to be a small metal box." Harper scraped away a little more dirt with his hands to gain access. The water over the years had rusted the square box to the point that flakes of metal fell from it as Harper pulled it from the ground. "It's not very heavy."

"How much could Spanish coins weigh?" I asked.

"I've no idea."

"Can you remove the lid?"

"The box is pretty rusted. Do you have a screwdriver so I can pry open the lid?" Harper asked as he moved the metal box to the patio table.

"I've got some tools in the laundry room. I'll be right back." I rummaged through my supply drawer and returned with a screwdriver in hand. "Here you go." I gave it to Harper.

Harper carefully placed the tip of the screwdriver along the seam of the lid to the box and slowly pried the lid loose. He carefully lifted the lid and inside we spied a small burlap bag. He gently lifted the aged bag out of the container. Twine was tightly wrapped around the top of the bag to keep the contents secure. He pulled out his pocket knife and cut the twine, holding the bag closed, then opened the bag.

I anxiously peered inside at several coins. I stared in amazement. "We actually found the coins that almost cost us our lives."

Harper dumped the contents of the bag in his hand. "You were right. Here are the coins that Dorothy and her husband hid so many years ago. What do we do with them now that we have found them?"

"Good question. I'm sure they must be worth quite a bit of money. They belonged to Dorothy, though. It doesn't feel right to keep them."

"You don't have to decide right away. Walter, Jr. is the only one alive that knows anything about them and he is in prison. Let's find some place safe to hide them and you can decide later. I'll put the yard back the way it was so no one will ask any questions."

I carried the coins into the house. "Well, Dorothy, you did it. You managed to catch your killer and show me where you buried your treasure from the grave. Now what do you want me to do with them?" I hesitated, half expecting Dorothy's ghost to reappear and answer my question. No such luck. All was quiet except for Max panting in the kitchen waiting for me to refill his water dish.

"I'm sorry Max. I got so distracted with my hunt for treasure that I forgot to get you some water after our walk." I filled his bowl full of water and noticed his empty dog biscuit container on the shelf. That would be a perfect place to hide the coins. I had decorated an old, large pickle jar with paint and used it as a spare treat container for Max. I unscrewed the lid of the container and placed the coins inside. I tightly secured the lid back in place. No one would think to look there for valuables. With all the burglaries lately I want to make sure the coins are someplace no one would look.

I walked into the family room to find Harper collapsed on the sofa, cooling off from our walk and digging up my front yard. "I found a safe place for the coins." I held the jar up so he could see. "I am going to place it in the utility room, on the shelf next to Max's dog food. Just in case something happens to me I want to make sure you know where they are hidden."

"Don't talk like that. Nothing is going to happen to you."

"The way things have been going lately, you never know."

"I can't imagine a burglar would look in the utility room for any valuables," Harper said.

"Can I get you something to drink?" I asked him.

"Some sweet tea would be great."

I returned with two glasses of sweet tea and joined him on the sofa to relax and cool off. "How is your side doing?"

"It's starting to itch so it must mean it's healing. I should probably go clean it to make sure it doesn't get infected. How are your wrists feeling?" He tenderly touched them.

"They're fine. It will just take some time for the bruising to disappear." To brighten the mood I asked, "Do you need some help in the shower?" I gave Harper my wicked grin. He pulled me to him and kissed me passionately. We showered together, washing each other's back. Harper caressed me as I tried to gently clean his wound. Still soaking wet we fell into the bed where we made love. It was different from before. The love we felt had been strengthened by the fact we had almost lost each other this week. Being reminded of how precious each day we have together made our love making that much more intense. Still exhausted from the events of the week, we fell asleep in each other's arms.

# Sixteen

The wet nose of my precious golden retriever pressed against my face along with the weight of his arms across my chest, woke me from a splendidly peaceful sleep. Max was ready to get up and anxiously waited for me to move. I slowly opened my eyes and smiled at my beloved friend. At the first sign of life, Max jumped off the bed and ran, barking happily, to the door to go for his morning walk. I knew Harper needed to get ready for work so there was no need to keep Max quiet.

"What time is it?" Harper groggily asked.

"It's seven o'clock."

"Man, I really crashed last night. I guess it was all that good food your mom fed me yesterday."

"Oh, and don't forget all the energy you expended finding the Spanish coins."

"I think it had more to do with the energy I expended after that in the shower!" Harper smiled and leaned over to kiss me.

"If you keep that up you'll be late for work."

Harper rolled over on top of me and started kissing me all over.

I started to giggle and Max barked wildly to remind me he was waiting. "All right boy, I'm coming." Begrudgingly Harper freed me from his grasp. I scurried out of bed and quickly dressed in shorts, t-shirt and running shoes. I attached Max's leash to his collar and headed for the door. "I won't be long," I yelled to Harper.

Harper smiled to himself as he watched Maggie run out the door. He realized how lucky he was to have her in his life. He found the energy to crawl out of bed and dress for work. He walked down to the kitchen to grab a bite to eat before he left. He was eating a bowl of cereal when Max came rushing through the door in a mad dash to his food bowl.

"How was your walk?"

"Well, we didn't run into any more cats, thank goodness." I poured Max some dry dog food and a large bowl of water. He devoured his breakfast within seconds.

"Can I make you some coffee before you leave?" I asked Harper.

"No, I'm running late as it is. I'll grab a cup of coffee once I get to work. You have fun with my Mom today."

"Oh, I forgot I'm supposed to meet her for lunch. Thanks for reminding me."

Harper put his cereal bowl in the kitchen sink and gave me a quick kiss before rushing out the door. As soon as the door closed I felt a sense of emptiness. I didn't feel complete without Harper by my side. I quickly came out of my daydream at the sound of the phone ringing.

"Hello."

"Did I wake you dear?"

"No Mom, I just got back from walking Max."

"Good. Do you have time to shop for a wedding dress today?"

"I'm meeting Harper's Mom for lunch. I can meet you after that if you like."

"Do you mind if I pick up some sample wedding stationary for you to view? We need to have them made today if they are going to be received in time for the wedding."

I rolled my eyes and bit the inside of my cheek, trying to remain calm. "Please Mom, just keep it simple."

"How about I pick you up at two? There are several bridal shops I want to take you to."

"All right, I'll see you at two." I knew there was no arguing with my Mom once she had her mind made up. It's just simpler to let her do things her way.

I called Sylvia's house to see what time to pick up Helen for lunch. We agreed to meet at eleven to talk wedding plans while we ate at Gator Landing on the river.

By the time I grabbed a quick bite to eat for breakfast, took a pleasantly long, warm shower, and dressed in a spaghetti strap cotton flowered dress, with a white long sleeve cotton jacket to cover my wrists, it was time to drive to Sylvia's house to pick up Helen. I was a little nervous, which I knew was unwarranted. I wanted to make a good impression on my future mother-in-law.

Helen quickly put me at ease. "You look lovely, dear. I know why Harper is so in love with you."

"Well, thank you," I blushed.

On the way to the restaurant I asked about Harper's childhood.

"Harper was always more mature than kids his age. After his father left I think Harper felt the burden of being the only man in the house. I worked a lot, trying to pay the bills, so Harper and Sylvia were alone several hours after school each night. I never had to worry about them getting into trouble. Harper was a good boy. As he grew older he loved working with his hands and fixing things. I would come home and my washing machine would be disassembled and parts laying all over the garage floor. Do you know what Harper said when I asked him why he took my washing machine apart?"

"I can only imagine," I replied.

"He said he heard a squeak when the drum rotated and thought he would fix it," Helen laughed. "I want you to know that he had the machine back together before he went to bed and it worked perfectly and no longer squeaked."

I could see the pride on Helen's face as she talked about her son. During lunch we discussed where to have the rehearsal dinner. "My Dad belongs to the Moose Lodge and their building should hold more than we plan to invite. I don't think there will be more than fifty people at the rehearsal dinner, depending on how many family members you want to attend."

"I don't think any of Harper's aunts or uncle will attend, so it will probably just be me and Sylvia's family from my side."

"How many brothers and sisters do you have?"

"I have two sisters and one brother who live all over the country from California to Virginia. With their busy schedules and the short notice I don't see that they will be able to travel here for the wedding."

"Well, that's too bad. I'll have to make sure we send them some pictures or a video of the ceremony. How about food? Does BBQ sound okay? We can order the BBQ and all the fixins from a local restaurant."

"Harper loves BBQ, so that will work nicely. I'll take care of the decorations."

After lunch I took Helen to my store. Since it was closed on Mondays we had the place to ourselves. She seemed genuinely impressed with what I had created. I looked at my watch and was shocked at the time. "I hate to rush you, but I have plans to meet my mom at two to go wedding dress shopping."

"I understand and I'm glad we had this time to get to know each other better. I know you are going to make Harper very happy."

On the way to Sylvia's house Helen discussed the few people she wanted to invite to the wedding. "I couldn't afford a big wedding when Sylvia got married, so we kept it simple. She looked like a princess, though, when she walked down the aisle. I understand your Mom's desire to make this day special for you."

"I know you would like to spend some more time with Harper before you leave. Why don't you plan to come to my house for supper tomorrow? I'll tell Harper to pick you up after work."

"That would be lovely."

"I'm not the best cook, so don't expect much!"

"I was a horrible cook when I first got married. Don't worry, you'll learn over time."

I dropped Helen off and raced to my house to meet Mom who was probably steaming by now. As I expected, Mom was sitting in her car in front of my house when I arrived. "I'm sorry Mom, lunch ran over. Hopefully you haven't been waiting long."

"We need to hurry. I made you an appointment at a wedding salon for two thirty to try on dresses."

I rolled my eyes. "Remember Mom, we want to keep the wedding simple."

"There is no reason you can't look like a princess when you walk down the aisle. Most every girl dreams of their wedding day to be just like a childhood fairy tale."

I smiled to myself as I remembered dressing up with my girlfriends in their Mom's fancy clothes, imagining the day I got married. "You're right. I just don't want you to go into debt over this wedding."

"Don't worry about the cost. You only get married once."

The rest of the afternoon I tried on what seemed like fifty wedding dresses and modeled them for Mom. Of course the first one I tried on was my favorite and I was ready to leave. Mom wouldn't hear of it, though. She was sure I would find something I liked more. Finally, after two hours of trying on every style of wedding dress, Mom agreed the first one I modeled for her looked the best on me. Next we shopped for shoes. I wanted something practical with a low heel so I wouldn't trip walking down the aisle. Mom wanted me to wear high heel satin shoes with sequins.

"This shoe looks so elegant. It will make you taller and appear more slender."

I tried not to take her comment as an insult but it was hard. "Mom, you're the one always trying to fatten me up because you say I look too skinny. Now I'm too fat?"

"It's just until you're married and then you can eat whatever you want. You don't want to look heavy in your wedding pictures."

I found myself biting the inside of my cheek again so I wouldn't lash out at Mom. Finally done for the day, Mom dropped me off at my house. Before I could get out of the car she lectured me on everything I needed to do tomorrow. Without a word I stepped out of the car and walked inside. I was greeted by Max and Harper. I must have looked a fright.

"You have this glazed over look in your eye. Why don't you sit down?"

"You have no idea how much restraint it took for me not to kill my Mother today." I collapsed on the sofa.

"How did lunch go with my Mom?"

"Oh, that went great! You have the best Mom. Do you want to trade?"

"I don't think your Dad would approve," Harper laughed.

I went over the events of the day, then shared what Mom had planned for me for tomorrow. "Somehow, while running my shop, my Mom thinks I am going to have all this free time to run around town with her. I will try to take a long lunch and have Gloria cover the store while I try to appease my Mom. Oh, before I forget, I invited your Mom for supper tomorrow night."

"That was nice of you." Harper kissed me. "Did you have any plans for food tonight?"

"I'm not that hungry after pigging out at lunch with your Mom. What can I fix you?"

"How about I order a pizza?"

"Just buy enough for you. My Mom told me I was fat and I better watch what I eat until the wedding."

"Don't be ridiculous! You're not fat." Harper reached over to pinch my waist. "See there's hardly anything there to grab. I like my women more meaty." Harper puffed up his chest and pretended to be a cave man. He had me laughing until I almost cried. I quickly forgot about my Mom and enjoyed the evening with Harper.

***

The next two weeks flew by. After surviving the rehearsal dinner on Thursday, my quilting club wanted to throw me a bachelorette party Friday evening. I was not sure what to expect.

At five o'clock I turned off the open sign just as a stretch limo pulled in front of the store. The door on the limo opened and Sylvia stepped out.

"Hurry up girl, we have a big night planned!" Sylvia grabbed my arm and shoved me in the back of the limo.

I looked around and was surprised to see everyone from the quilting club was there. Gloria, Audrey, Valerie, Cynthia, Joanne and Celia all had mischievous smiles on their faces. "Celia, I am so glad you didn't have to work."

"I worked all day so I could have the evening off. I didn't want to miss your bachelorette party."

Celia and I had become close after the role she played in saving my life. We talked frequently and she had become a regular at the quilting club. Joanne helped prepare Celia for a job interview by showing her how to dress more professional. The excessive blue eye shadow and red streaks through her hair were now gone. She had hidden her beauty behind her tight clothes and bright make-up. Celia interviewed for an administrative assistant position at a local car dealership and received a job offer right away. She, of course was ecstatic and accepted immediately. She had already set a goal for herself to become a saleswoman once she learned the business. It was so good to see Celia happy and on the right path to making a good future for herself.

"Audrey and Valerie, how were you able to escape your husbands and kids tonight?"

Audrey spoke up first. "I told Tom to have a guys night out with the boys. They were going for pizza and then down to the river to fish until dark."

"I convinced Chuck he would be rewarded if he looked after the kids tonight." Valerie winked at me. "If you know what I mean!" Everyone laughed at Valerie's innuendo.

"So where are we headed?" I pried.

"That's a surprise," Sylvia said. "Let's start this party while we let the driver take us to our destination. Anyone care for a drink?" Sylvia held up a bottle of merlot she retrieved from a compartment in the limo. Everyone grabbed a wine glass and Sylvia found a corkscrew to open the wine bottle. It was not long before we were all giggling from the effects of the wine.

We arrived at our destination in Orlando around seven. The limo parked in front of a rustic looking restaurant. I could hear reggae music playing in the distance. We entered the restaurant which was decorated in a Caribbean theme. There were large bamboo ceiling fans circulating throughout the restaurant. We followed our hostess to an outdoor eating area with a tiki bar. The view was stupendous, overlooking a serene lake. The band was located on a wooden deck and serenaded the crowd with joyous music. We were escorted to our table that had been reserved for us outside on the patio. The large, wooden, round table had a coconut centerpiece. There were strings of brightly colored tropical pineapple lights hanging from an overhead canopy and sand placed along the shore of the lake to give you the feel of being on the beach. The atmosphere was very festive. The waitress took our drink orders after there was much discussion of which tropical drinks to try first.

"Everything on the menu looks scrumptious," I said. "How did you hear about this place?"

"John brought me here for our wedding anniversary this year," Sylvia said. "I thought this would be the perfect place to relax and enjoy yourself before your big day tomorrow."

"I love it. I'll have to bring Harper here some time."

We started with some appetizers of poppers and fried cheese. Our drinks arrived and the volume increased as we laughed the night away. We were on our second round of drinks by the time our meals arrived. The food was awesome. We sampled each other's plates to taste the different food choices offered. By the time we devoured our meals and dessert we were all stuffed.

"I'm never going to be able to fit into my wedding dress tomorrow."

"I've an idea of how we can work off some of that food. The music is calling." Audrey stood up and grabbed my hand pulling me to the dance floor. Audrey held her arms above her head and started swaying to the Jamaican music as the drums beat to the rhythm. We all joined in laughing as we danced together. Before I knew it, it was after midnight and we were all danced out.

"Hey guys, I hate to be the party pooper but I've got to get up early tomorrow for my wedding."

"Oh my gosh, look at the time. Where did the evening go?" Sylvia said. "I only have the limo until two, so we better hurry."

We exited the restaurant and looked around for our ride home. "There's our limo," Valerie said as she pointed toward the back of the parking lot.

We approached the limo and tried the doors. They were locked. Sylvia walked around to the driver's side and peered in the window. "That's strange there's no one inside. He was supposed to wait for us to return and drive us home."

"Do you think he got tired of waiting and went inside to get something to eat?" Cynthia asked.

"You guys stay here and I'll check." Sylvia disappeared inside the restaurant.

"I hope she hurries I'm getting eaten alive by mosquitos," Valerie said as she swatted her arms.

"Does anyone have a hair pin?" Celia asked.

Cynthia pulled a pin from her hair and handed it to Celia.

"What do you plan to do with that?" I asked.

"I can at least open the door to the limo so we have somewhere comfortable to sit while we wait for Sylvia to return."

Before I had a chance to object, I heard the door click. Celia opened the door, "Voila!"

"Where did you learn to do that?" Cynthia asked.

Celia handed her hair pin back to Cynthia. "Just something I picked up," Celia said. No one but Joanne and I knew about Celia's past.

We climbed inside the comfort of the limo and waited for Sylvia to return. Joanne spoke up, "I forgot we have some wedding shower gifts for you in the trunk. Celia, can you climb in the front seat and pull the lever to open the trunk?"

Celia stepped out of the limo and slipped into the front seat looking for the lever to open the trunk. "Here it is," she proudly announced. The trunk popped open. We all climbed out of the limo and walked to the back to retrieve the presents.

We stopped dead in our tracks when we spied what was inside the trunk. It was a body. "I think we found our limo driver," I said.

"Is he alive?" Cynthia asked.

After some hesitation Joanne reached for the neck of the body and felt for a pulse. "I don't feel a pulse. We better call the police." We all suddenly became very sober.

"All right everyone, remain calm," I said. "I am sure there has to be a logical explanation for his demise."

Joanne dialed 911 and talked to the operator.

Sylvia walked up. "I had him paged, and walked around the bar, but couldn't find him anywhere. Why do all of you have that strange look on your faces?"

"Unfortunately, we found him." I pointed toward the trunk.

"Oh my word, what happened?"

"Celia opened the trunk so we could retrieve the wedding shower gifts and this is what we found."

"Are the gifts still in there?" Sylvia asked.

"We find a dead body in the trunk of our limo and that's the question you ask, seriously?"

"Well, I think you'll really like what I bought for you."

"I'm sure I will, but right now me opening my presents is the least of our worries."

Valerie peered inside the trunk and looked past the gruesome body. "Yes, the presents are still there, but the dead guy is laying on some of them."

142

"That's nice. I think I'll pass on my wedding shower gifts for now and let the police sort it out."

Celia pulled a cigarette out of her purse and stepped away from the group before lighting it. I watched as she inhaled deeply. I walked over to her to see if she was okay. "I haven't seen you smoke since, you know that day. Are you all right?"

"This is just too reminiscent of my past life. Do you think Roy could have been released from prison?"

"No. Roy should be behind bars for a long time. This must have something to do with whatever the limo driver was into."

I heard Sylvia talking to the limo company. She explained to the person at the other end of the line about our predicament. After what seemed like a lengthy conversation she ended the call.

"Well, what did they say?" I asked.

"The person on the other end of the phone was understandably upset about their driver. She explained that all the limos had been reserved for the night and no one was available to take us home. She offered to get us a hotel and have someone take us home in the morning."

"Did you tell her I was getting married tomorrow and needed to get home tonight?"

"Yes, she apologized, but there was nothing more she could do."

"What do we do now?" Valeria asked?

"I'll call John," Sylvia said. "He can pick us up in my van. Harper can watch over the boys while John is gone." While Sylvia phoned John, the police arrived with their blue lights blinding us. After the police confirmed that there was truly a dead body in the trunk and we hadn't made it up in our drunken stupor, we were each interviewed separately. After explaining what little we knew they finally allowed us to leave.

"Oh, Mr. Officer would it be possible to retrieve the wedding gifts from the trunk?" Sylvia politely asked.

"I'm sorry ma'am, but they will have to be confiscated as evidence for now."

143

"Wonderful! Maggie, this will definitely be a bachelorette party you will never forget."

"Oh Sylvia, there was no way for you to know our limo driver was going to be murdered." I tried to improve everyone's mood. "I couldn't have dreamed of a better way to spend my bachelorette party, than with all my friends. I had so much fun tonight with y'all eating and dancing the night away. We can continue the celebration tomorrow at my reception."

John finally arrived and we all squeezed into Sylvia's van around 3 AM. It was a quiet ride home. The alcohol buzz had worn off and everyone was beyond tired.

I arrived home at 5 AM and crawled into bed. Max was staying with Harper at Sylvia's house so I had the house to myself. I set my alarm for 9 AM. I figured that would give me enough time to prepare for my wedding, scheduled to start at 1:00 PM. Even though I was exhausted, when I closed my eyes all I saw was the dead limo driver in the trunk staring back at me. I finally drifted off to sleep as the sun was just starting to rise. I awoke suddenly to the phone ringing.

"Hello," I mumbled into the receiver in my half awake state.

"Mom. What do you mean where am I?"

"You're supposed to be getting married in thirty minutes."

I glanced over at my clock. That can't be right. I blinked to clear my eyes. The clock indicated it was 12:30 PM. "Crap! My alarm didn't go off! I'll throw everything in the car and dress at the church." I slammed down the phone, took a thirty-second shower and threw on shorts and a t-shirt. I pulled my hair back into a ponytail and threw all my hair products and make-up in a duffel bag. I ran out of the house with my wedding dress draped over my arm, wedding shoes in one hand, car keys in the other with a duffel bag of beauty supplies draped over my shoulder, barefoot. I made record time to the church and was greeted by Mom in the parking lot.

"You look a wreck. What happened to you last night at your bachelorette party?"

144

"I don't have time to explain right now Mom. Can you please just help me get ready?"

"Of course, dear. Let's me help you with your dress."

Sylvia met me at the door looking gorgeous in her peach maid of honor gown. "I should have called you this morning to make sure you were up. I'm sorry."

"It's not your fault my alarm didn't go off. Can you help do my hair while I work on my make-up?"

"You got it." Sylvia removed the band from my hair letting the frizzy mess fall to my shoulders. She took the curling iron and started making soft curls around my face. She French braided the back and then wrapped my hair in a bun pinning it in place.

I quickly finished my make-up and stepped into my wedding gown. Mom zipped up the back while I slipped into my white high heel satin shoes. I smelled under my arms then showered myself in perfume. I fanned my flush, sweating face and tried to catch my breath. Ready or not, it was time to get married.

"What is holding up the show?" Grandma asked as she peeked into my dressing room. "Everyone is starting to think the bride jumped ship."

"I'm ready, Grandma."

Mom grabbed my hand. "You look beautiful darling. Your Dad is waiting for you at the back of the church to walk you down the aisle."

I took a deep breath and slowly released it. This is really happening, I thought.

"When Harper sees how gorgeous you are he is going to be speechless," Sylvia said.

The organ music started. I smiled as I watched the flower girl in her pink dress and bow tied hair along with the ring bearer in his little tux walk down the aisle hand in hand. Sylvia followed leaving just Dad and me standing in the vestibule alone.

"You have turned into such a beautiful young lady," Dad said as he took my hand and placed it around his arm.

I made the mistake of looking into my Dad's eyes. My strong, always in control Dad was holding back tears. "Oh Dad, I love you so much!" I stood on my tiptoes and kissed Dad on the cheek as a tear ran down my face.

"You will always be my baby girl, no matter how old you are." The wedding march music started to play. "Are you ready?"

I wiped the tear from my cheek and we entered the sanctuary. I couldn't believe my eyes. The church was packed. I glanced down the aisle toward the front of the church to where Harper stood. He looked so handsome in his white tux standing next to his brother-in-law, John. Sylvia smiled back at me as I approached and I handed her my bouquet. Harper took my hands in his as the minister started, "We are gathered here today to witness the union of Maggie Thompson and Harper McGillan." The rest was a blur. I remember saying, "I do." But, that's about it. Before I knew it, I was married and the minister was saying, "You may now kiss the bride." Harper pulled me to him and kissed me lovingly in front my family and friends. It felt different now that we were married. A calm came over me knowing Harper would always be by my side and give me the strength and confidence to face whatever challenges lie ahead.

Following the ceremony, the wedding photographer took so many shots I could no longer feel my face from smiling so much. Finally, we arrived at the reception. My parents had spent a fortune to make sure everyone enjoyed themselves. The disc jockey had the crowd already dancing to the music by the time we arrived. Everyone looked to be having a good time. I clung to Harper as we made our way through the crowd, visiting with our guests. I finally got a second to stop and talk to some of the women that were at the bachelorette party with me the previous night. "I'm so glad you all made it. I wasn't sure you would after getting in so late last night."

"We started to wonder the same about you!" Cynthia chimed in.

146

I explained about my alarm not going off and everyone had a good laugh at my expense. "Where is Celia? Last night she told me she had the day off from work and planned to attend the wedding today. Has anyone seen her?"

"The last time I saw her was when she left my place in her car to drive home early this morning," Sylvia said.

"Maybe she overslept like you. I'll try calling her at the women's shelter to make sure she made it home safely," Joanne said.

I was a little concerned since Celia was so quiet during the ride home last night. I know seeing the limo driver dead shook her up a little bit. "Joanne, will you please give me a call when you reach Celia to let me know she is okay?"

"Of course, but the only thing you need to be worrying about is your honeymoon." All the women laughed.

Harper appeared as if on cue. "I think it's time for us to dance." Harper held out his hand for me to take hold of. He was nervous about dancing in front of everyone. We had been practicing in the living room each night for the past week so he wouldn't step on my toes. He held me close and led me around the dance floor like we practiced, but it was much more intimate this time. As the music stopped he held me tightly and whispered in my ear, "Dancing with you is like making love, every move brings us closer together."

I blushed, but knew what he meant. I was ready for our honeymoon to begin. We cut our cakes and Harper didn't cram the piece in my face as I had feared. We said our quick good-byes and were pelted by birdseed as we left the reception to start our new life together. An hour later we arrived at our hotel on the beach near St. Augustine.

Harper stopped me from entering the room. "Wait, I've got to do this right." He lifted me off the ground and carried me across the threshold as I giggled. He closed the door with his foot and threw me on the bed. He started kissing me all over. Our love making was interrupted by my cell phone ringing.

"Oh, I better get that. I told Joanne to call me when she found Celia," I told Harper. "Hello. Joanne, did you talk to Celia?"

"I hate to call and ruin your honeymoon, but I talked to the women at the shelter and Celia never arrived home last night. Her bed was not slept in. Do you think she went back to her old life?"

"She would never do that. You saw how happy she was working at the car dealership and partying with us last night. I'm worried that one of Roy's goons may have tracked her down. You saw how nervous she was last night after we discovered the limo driver was dead. Can you contact the police and see what they can do?"

"I can, but since she is eighteen and free to do as she pleases, I'm sure they won't do anything without evidence of some crime being committed."

"I've a bad feeling about this, Joanne. You know what battered women go through. Their self esteem is torn down so their abuser can keep them under control. I know Celia would never go back willingly."

"Let me do some checking around to see what I can find out. Try not to worry and enjoy your honeymoon. I'll call as soon as I discover what has happened."

I hung up the phone and explained my concern to Harper. He kissed me on the forehead and told me, "Don't worry. I am sure after last night she just crashed at a friend's house or something."

"That's just it. All her old friends were Roy's friends. We are her friends now."

"Why don't we take a walk down the beach and see if there is someplace close to get a bite to eat? I didn't get a chance to eat much at our reception and I am starved."

I laughed. "All that food and we didn't even get a chance to enjoy any of it. I am sure Mom will save us some cake for when we get home."

We walked hand in hand, enjoying the warm breeze off the ocean, talking about the wedding. Harper pointed out the lights from a bar and grill just off the beach and we headed towards it.

We sat at a table outside, enjoying the ocean view. While we waited for our food I couldn't help thinking about Celia. My cell phone rang and I answered it quickly. It was Joanne.

"I called the police to report my concern about Celia and they informed me that Roy made bail."

"That's not good. He has to be the one that has Celia. I'm sure that as soon as he got out of prison he hunted her down."

"That's my fear, too. The police are going to track Roy down and ask him about Celia. But even if the police find him and ask him about Celia he will never admit to the police he has her."

"If Roy somehow found out that Celia was the one that let me go that night in the abandoned church he won't hesitate to kill her."

"Try not to worry. This is supposed to be the happiest day of your life. I will let you know if there is any news."

I hung up the phone and relayed the latest information to Harper. The food we had ordered was delivered but I had lost my appetite. I picked at my food while Harper devoured his meal and some of mine too. We walked back to the room as it was getting dark. The sound of the waves gently crashing against the shore calmed my nerves.

Harper stopped walking and turned me toward him. He lifted my chin up and looked into my eyes. "Stop worrying, they will find her," he said. Then his lips pressed against mine and he wrapped his arms tightly around me. I just wanted to get lost in Harper's arms and forget all about my troubles. We returned to our room.

"To help you relax, how about I give you a massage?" Harper asked.

"Oh, that sounds heavenly. Is that one of the benefits of being married?" I asked, smiling wickedly.

He started rubbing my shoulders and unlatched my bra so he could caress my back. It wasn't long before we were making passionate love. We both fell asleep in each other's arms, exhausted from the day's events.

Suddenly I was aware of not being able to move. I opened my eyes to total blackness around me. My wrists and legs were bound. I tried to scream but the gag in my mouth only allowed a muffled noise. The heat and retched smell was all around me. I started to panic when the door opened allowing just enough light for me to see who was standing at the door. It was Roy. I struggled to get loose and screamed before he could hurt me again.

"Maggie, wake up! You're having a nightmare!"

I struggled to get-a-way from my attacker.

"Maggie, it's Harper."

Harper put his arms around me to stop me from struggling with him. I sobbed into his shoulders after having such a vivid nightmare. It seemed so real.

"You are safe." Harper held me tightly until my sobs subsided. "You're soaking wet with perspiration. Are you all right?"

Before I could answer I started to shake uncontrollably with chills. Harper wrapped the covers around my shoulders. "I was back in that closet, locked in the church, not able to move." I wiped the tears from my face as I recalled the nightmare.

"Let me get you some water."

I held on tightly to the blanket wrapped around me.

"Here, drink this."

I gulped down the water. Harper wrapped his arms back around me to stop me from shaking.

It was killing Harper to see me in such distress, knowing there was nothing he could do to take away my pain other than to just be there for me. "Are you feeling better?" he asked.

"Yes." I finally stopped trembling and dried the tears from my eyes. "I am so fortunate to have you for a husband." I reached for Harper's hand and held it tightly. "I think my nightmare was trying to tell me something."

"What could reliving your horrible attack have possibly told you?"

150

"Maybe Roy is holding Celia in the same place he hid me, in the abandoned church." I pushed back the covers to get out of bed.

"It's 5 AM. Where do you think you're going?"

"I've got to see if she is there."

Harper grabbed my wrist to stop me. "You're going to do no such thing. If Roy sees you he won't hesitate to kill you. Call the police and have them check the church. They can get there much faster than we can. If Celia is there they can rescue her."

I hated to admit it but, "I guess you're right." Harper release dmy wrist now that I was acting more rational.

"You stay put and I will call the police to have them check the church for Celia." Harper picked up his cell phone by the bed and dialed the Palatka Police Department.

While Harper called the police I called Joanne and shared my theory. Joanne agreed it would be like Roy to take Celia someplace he was familiar with and that crime scene tape would not stop him from entering the church. She couldn't believe she hadn't thought of it herself.

Harper ended his call. "The police are going to send a squad car to check the church and let us know if they find Celia. There is nothing we can do for now. Why don't you try to get some more rest?"

"There is no way I can fall back to sleep now. How about I make us some coffee and we can go out on the balcony and watch the sunrise while we wait for the phone to ring?"

"That sounds nice." Harper was exhausted from the last few days but knew I needed his support. He dragged himself out of bed and joined me on the balcony.

I handed Harper a mug of hot coffee and pulled him toward me so he would join me on the large lounge chair. We cuddled together to stay warm from the cool breeze blowing off the ocean. We listened to the sound of the waves gently crashing along the shoreline and watched as the lights of a ship made its way northward. We sat quietly holding hands, enjoying the serene beauty in front of us. We became lost in our own thoughts as the sky turned lighter. The sun pierced through the clouds along the horizon, flooding the sky with pink and orange rays, giving us a day of hope for things to come.

# Seventeen

After two mugs of coffee I could hear Harper's stomach growling. "How about we get dressed and wander down to the lobby for a bite to eat for breakfast?"

Harper leaned over, kissed me deeply, and started to caress me. "I have a better idea. How about we go back to bed, you let me make passionate love to you, and then we get something to eat?"

"How can I resist such a proposal?" I laughed.

Harper scooped me into his arms and threw me on the bed, still giggling. He smothered my mouth with his and kissed me longingly.

After making love and taking a warm shower together, we dressed and made our way to the breakfast buffet. At the sight of all the choices I exclaimed, "I'm starved!" My Mom's words suddenly came back to me. *"You can eat as much as you want after you're married."* I laughed to myself as I decided on a breakfast of waffles and a blueberry muffin.

We found a table and I stared at the mound of food on my plate. I took a large mouthful of waffle first. "Umm, this breakfast will definitely add a few pounds to my waistline," I shared with Harper.

"I don't think you have anything to worry about," Harper said with a mouthful of eggs and bacon.

After eating ourselves to the point of misery I suggested, "How about we go relax by the pool?" I was too tired and full to do anything more than lay around in a stupor.

"Sounds like a stupendous plan," Harper joked as he rubbed his full tummy.

Dressed in my cotton flowered shorts and strapless top we found two lounge chairs that were partially in the shade so the sun wouldn't bake us. The warmth of the sun and soft noise of waves in the distance quickly had me drifting off to sleep. My cell phone suddenly rang, bringing me out of my slumber. I jumped to grab it and hurriedly answered, "Joanne, did you find her?"

"Yes, you were right. Celia was locked in the closet of the abandoned church."

I could tell by her tone it was not good. "Is she all right?" I cautiously asked.

"She is still alive, but barely. She was brutally beaten, and unconscious when the police found her. I'm at the hospital now. The doctors are still evaluating her condition."

"I'm on my way."

"Now hold on. There is nothing you can do for Celia. She's in good hands. Once the doctors have completed their exam I will call and let you know her status. All you can do now is say a prayer for her."

"I should be there with her. She saved my life and I feel like I let her down." Tears started to well up in my eyes.

"There is nothing you could have done to stop this. The police are looking for Roy and you're safer where you are until he is captured and locked back up. You only get one honeymoon. Enjoy your day with Harper and I will see you tomorrow. I'll call as soon as there is any word on Celia's condition."

I ended the call and explained to Harper what little I knew. He wrapped his arms around me to comfort me. I buried my face in his chest to hide my tears. Harper knew I needed time to process what had happened. He held me quietly. The sound of the waves must have lulled me back to sleep. I awoke to the glare of the sun in my face. I shielded my eyes and glanced over at Harper, sleeping soundly. His skin was starting to take on the red appearance of a baked lobster. I hated to wake him but knew we would both be in agony tonight if we didn't get out of the sun. I gently kissed him to bring him out of his deep sleep.

He slowly opened his eyes and smiled up at me. "What time is it?"

"It's after one. We'd better retreat indoors before we get any redder." I pressed my thumb into his chest to show him that he was done.

We returned to our room to freshen up. I called Joanne to get the latest status on Celia.

Joanne didn't have much good news to share. "She is still unconscious and the doctors are not sure when she may wake up. There is a large lump on her head along with many lacerations to her face and body. She is also very dehydrated from being locked in the hot church for several hours."

I remembered the oppressive heat when I was trapped in the closet. If it hadn't been for Celia letting me out, I would have died from heat exhaustion. "Give me a call when she wakes up or if there is any change in her condition."

Harper suggested playing tourist the rest of the afternoon to keep my mind off Celia. We stopped at a grill located on the beach and both ate a large hamburger and fries. "I don't know why I have such a ferocious appetite today."

Harper teased me with his smile. "I bet I know!"

"You are too much," I joked in exasperation.

After lunch we burned off our hamburgers by walking up 219 stairs of the spiral staircase leading to the top of the St. Augustine lighthouse. "I don't think my legs will ever be the same," I exclaimed as I stepped on the last step.

The pain was worth it. "Wow, what a breathtaking view!" I stepped up to the rail and looked down to see how far we had climbed.

"Do you really think you should stand so close to the edge?" Harper asked.

I turned around to see Harper pressed up against the wall of the lighthouse.

"Are you afraid of heights?"

"No, I'm afraid of falling."

"Nonsense, this railing is secure." I pressed against the aluminum post to show him it was safe and held out my hand to him. He grabbed it and joined me in admiring the breathtaking view.

After making our way back down the lighthouse stairs, we drove to the Castillo de San Marcos Fort. It is the oldest fort made from coquina in the continental United States. We inspected the rooms used to house prisoners during the Revolutionary War. I could feel the spirits of the past occupants as I imagined how harsh life must have been for them.

Evening quickly approached and we finished our tour by window-shopping in the historic downtown area and eating at a quaint Spanish restaurant. The day was perfect and I didn't want it to end. I hadn't heard from Joanne so I knew there was no change in Celia's condition.

The next morning while eating another monstrous breakfast I asked Harper, "Would you mind if we went home early? I know we planned to stay until this afternoon but I really want to go to the hospital to spend some time with Celia."

"I was going to suggest the same thing. You were very restless, tossing and turning most of the night. I know you won't be able to get a good night's rest until you see Celia for yourself."

I leaned over and kissed Harper softly on the lips. "You're so good to me. I am so lucky to have you as my husband."

"What can I say?" Harper gloated jokingly.

We packed our things and drove straight to the Palatka Medical Center. I walked in and stopped at the reception desk to ask for Celia's room number. I was informed that she was in intensive care and was not allowed any visitors. When I persisted and explained that I was a close friend I was informed that they could only provide her medical status to family members. All I was able to determine was that she was in stable condition. I pulled out my cell phone and dialed Joanne's number from the parking lot.

Joanne answered on the second ring. "Joanne I'm at the hospital but they won't let me see Celia," I angrily explained.

156

"I know. Celia listed me as her emergency point of contact at the women's shelter so the hospital is letting me visit her. There has really been no change in her condition. The doctors are cautiously optimistic that Celia will eventually wake up once the swelling goes down and when she is ready. Her injuries have all been treated and it's now just a matter of time."

"Can I go in with you to see her?"

"Yes, I see no reason why the hospital would stop you from visiting her if I accompanied you. I'm currently in the ICU waiting area."

"Great! I will see you shortly." Harper and I followed the signs to the ICU waiting area where I was greeted by Joanne.

"Wow, look at you! You definitely enjoyed the sun while you were on your honeymoon."

I hugged Joanne. "How are you holding up? You look exhausted."

"I stayed the night just in case Celia woke up. Let me see if the nurse will let us visit with her for a few minutes."

Joanne returned. "The nurse said we could stay with her for about fifteen minutes. I want to warn you though before we go in, Celia looks rough. Her arm is broken and her face is very swollen. You won't recognize her."

Harper squeezed my hand. "I'll wait here for you to return."

I braced myself and followed Joanne to where Celia was being monitored. I gasped at the sight of her. Celia's big brown eyes were swollen shut and her face was one big bruise. It looked like Roy had used her face as a punching bag. The respirator pumped air into Celia's lungs while machines monitoring her heart and blood pressure beeped. I pulled a chair up to Celia's bed and reached for her good hand. I gently squeezed her fingers. "Celia, it's Maggie and Joanne. You're safe and in the hospital. When you are ready to wake up we will be here for you."

I waited for a response but there was none. I watched her chest slowly rise up and down. I hoped wherever Celia was she was in no pain.

157

As if Joanne knew what I was thinking, she said. "They have her on some strong pain medicine right now. Hopefully the meds are allowing her to sleep peacefully. When she wakes up she is going to be in a lot of pain. Several of her teeth are missing and her jaw is broken."

Tears came to my eyes, then anger took over. "Have the police caught Roy yet?" I whispered in case Celia could hear me.

"No, they are still searching for him."

The nurse approached. "I'm sorry ladies, your time is up. You can visit again this evening if you like."

I hurriedly walked out of ICU. I could hardly breathe I was so furious with what Roy had done to such a kind-hearted, beautiful person. I've never felt such rage before in my life. How could another human being do such a thing? What Roy had done to me was nothing compared to what he had done to Celia.

I stormed out of the hospital with Harper racing after me. Harper grabbed my hand in the parking lot. "Slow down! What's your rush?" One look at my face told all. He pulled me into his arms. "You must have faith that God is with her. She is a strong girl and she will get through this with your help."

I wiped the tears from my face. "You're right, me falling apart is not going to help her. Let's go pick up Max from my parents and go home."

When we arrived at my parents house I opened the door and was run over by Max. He was so happy to see me. I kneeled down to his level and hugged him while he licked my face. Max gave love so freely that it brought a smile back to my face.

"Welcome home, you two!" Mom yelled as she walked into the family room. "I'm cooking a roast for supper if you would like to stay."

That's my Mom, always wanting to feed me. "Not tonight Mom, we are both tired and just want to get home and unpack."

"I understand. Maybe later in the week."

Max raced to the car, eager to make sure he was not left behind. When we arrived home Harper and I unloaded our bags, along with Max's food and belongings. Max, of course, went straight to the utility room to where his dog bowl is located. I gave him a little food and then noticed the dog biscuit jar where I placed the Spanish coins was missing. I frantically looked around the utility room to see if I had placed it on another shelf but there was no sign of it.

"Harper!" I yelled!

"Is everything all right?"

"No, the dog biscuit jar where I hid the Spanish coins is missing."

"Are you sure you didn't place it somewhere else?"

"No, I remember placing it right here where I store Max's food. I figured no one would look in here for anything of value."

"Well, the door was locked when we arrived home and there was no sign that anyone broke in. Could Dorothy's ghost have moved it?"

"I hadn't thought of that. But I haven't seen Dorothy since the night she helped catch Walter, Jr., her killer. I had hoped she was now resting peacefully."

"Do you want to call the police?"

"No, they would just think I've totally lost it. I would have to explain finding buried treasure in my front yard and then having it disappear. It's probably best if we keep our little secret to ourselves."

"I'm sure it will turn up. I've a more pressing matter on my mind at the moment. This is our first time in this house as husband and wife. Don't you think we should christen our marriage appropriately?" Harper pulled me toward him and kissed me longingly.

I soon forgot all about the missing coins. Harper managed to coerce me to bed, lost in each other's embrace.

# Eighteen

I visited Celia with Joanne for the next three days. After work on Thursday I sat by Celia's bed and held her hand like every other time and started to talk to her. "The guys at the car dealership are missing your smiling face. They hope you will return to work soon to brighten the showroom with your smiling face and help lighten their work load." Then I felt it. Celia's fingers moved. I lifted her hand and stared intently for any movement. Did I imagine it?

"What's wrong?" Joanne asked.

"I think I felt her fingers move!" I exclaimed. "Celia, if you can hear, me move your fingers." Joanne and I watched Celia's hand closely.

"Did you see that? She just moved her index finger!" I yelled.

Joanne raced to get a nurse.

"Celia, you can wake up now. Joanne and I are here with you." The swelling had gone down around her eyes enough to where she could open them. The respirator had been removed that morning and Celia was breathing on her own. Celia's eyes started to flicker. The nurse rushed in along with the doctor.

The doctor started to speak, "Just take your time Celia. You have been in an accident and are in the hospital."

Celia opened her eyes and blinked several times, trying to focus. I squeezed her hand. "Celia, it's Maggie. Don't be scared. You're safe."

Celia tried to talk but no words escaped her lips.

The nurse gave her some crushed ice to help lubricate her sore throat. "Is that better?"

Celia nodded cautiously.

"Can you tell me your name?" the doctor asked.

I held my breath as I waited for her to respond.

"Celia Riley," she whispered.

I exhaled and smiled, squeezing Celia's hand.

"How many fingers am I holding up?"

"Three."

"Correct. What color is my shirt?"

She hesitated and then said, "Purple?"

"Close enough. Would you like to suck on a little more ice?"

Celia slowly nodded her head up and down then stopped when the pain hit her. "Just take it slow," the nurse said as she held the glass to her lips so she could get a small piece of ice.

"I know it's difficult for you to talk. You have a pretty big bump on your head which is what is causing you the pain when you move your head. You have been unconscious for four days. You also have a broken arm, fractured jaw, and as you're probably aware are missing several teeth," the doctor explained.

A tear started to run down Celia's face.

"It's okay to cry, honey. You have been through Hell and back. Joanne and I will be here for you until you are ready to be on your own again."

The doctor continued, "It will take some time, but your body should heal with no permanent side effects. I know you're in a lot of pain and we will try to make you as comfortable as possible. Do you remember what happened to you?"

Celia quietly replied, "Yes."

"A police officer is waiting outside to ask you a few questions. Do you feel up to talking to him for just a few minutes?"

Celia looked up at me.

I squeezed her hand. "I am not going anywhere. I'll stay here with you."

She nodded shyly to the doctor. The nurse left the room to get the officer.

A young muscular police officer stepped into the room.

The doctor explained, "Celia needs her rest so you have just a few minutes to ask what you need."

"Understand. I won't take long," the officer replied.

The doctor stepped out of the room, along with the nurse. I continued to hold Celia's hand as the police officer looked into Celia eyes.

"My name is Calvin Kast. I know this will be difficult for you, but I need you to recall what happened. Can you remember the events of the night you were abducted?"

Celia calmly responded, "Yes. When I arrived at the women's shelter, after Maggie's bachelorette party, Roy and a few of his boys grabbed me as I was getting out of my car. A knife was held to my throat and I was told if I yelled I was dead." Celia lifted her good hand to her throat, feeling for a wound. She continued, "He must have found out where I was staying and was waiting for me to arrive."

"Do you know where Roy took you?"

"To the abandoned church downtown."

"Did he cause your injuries?"

Celia closed her eyes as she recalled being tortured. Tears started to stream down her face.

"I know this is difficult for you but I must know, did Roy cause all your injuries?" he asked again.

Celia finally answered softly, "Yes." She started to sob.

"Thank you, Miss Riley, for your help. I will make sure Roy never hurts anyone again. I will stop back by in a few days when you're a little stronger."

I saw true compassion in Calvin's eyes as he talked to Celia. "It's all right, honey. You have every reason to cry your eyes out after what you went through." I gently hugged Celia until she was all cried out.

***

The next day, Celia was moved out of ICU into a private room. The quilting club members took turns staying with Celia in the hospital each day and night to make sure she was never alone for a second. Her hospital room was full of balloons and flowers from her co-workers and people she had become acquainted with at the car dealership.

I kept Celia company Sunday night. Her strength and determination amazed me. She managed to joke about the hospital food and this morning was no different. "I could eat this oatmeal through a straw, it's so runny." The doctor walked in as she managed to eat a little of the oatmeal.

"Well, someone looks like they are feeling better today," the doctor said. "Can you tell me what your pain level is today?"

"It's a three." Celia announced with a convincing tone. She actual reduced it by a little bit, hoping she could be released if the doctor felt her pain level was improving. "Do you think I can leave today?"

The doctor joked as he looked at her chart. "What, you're not enjoying your stay here? Well, your numbers seemed to be holding steady and were good overnight. With your head injury you're going to have to take it easy for several more weeks. I will let you leave if you promise to get plenty of bedrest and don't push it too soon."

"I promise."

"A nurse will come with a wheelchair shortly to help you to your car."

The doctor left and we both shouted a muffled, "Yeah!"

Joanne had already brought Celia some clothes from her room at the women's center. I helped Celia get dressed. There was a quiet tap at the door.

"Come in !" I yelled.

It was Calvin Kast, the officer that had questioned Celia the day she woke up. "Well, it looks like you're feeling better."

This was the fourth time Calvin had stopped by to check on Celia. I knew his interest in Celia had to be more than just business. "I'm going to pull my car around," I told Celia. I wanted to give them some time alone.

163

When I returned Calvin was leaving and Celia was all smiles. "So what did he say?" I pried.

"He told me he was glad I was feeling better," Celia hesitated.

"And?"

"And he asked if he could continue to visit me."

"He likes you!"

"I don't know how. I must look atrocious."

"He must love damsels in distress. He can see through the bruises at what a beautiful person you really are inside and out."

"He also told me they have a lead on where Roy may be hiding out. He hoped he would be back in custody today."

"Speaking of that, Harper and I agree it's not safe for you to return to the women's shelter until Roy is captured. Plus, you need someone to take care of you until you're back on your feet. I've made up the guest room at my house so you can stay with us until you're well enough to take care of yourself, and Roy is back behind bars."

"I can't let you do that! You have done so much already. Y'all just got married. You need some time to yourselves."

"We won't take no for an answer. Harper and I have our entire lives to spend together."

The nurse came in with the wheelchair. We carefully supported Celia while she eased herself into the chair, wincing in pain. By the time we arrived at my house Celia was ready for a nap. I helped her settle into the guest room.  Just the little bit of exertion moving her to my house was enough to exhaust her and have her in agony again. I gave Celia a pain pill. It wasn't long before she fell asleep. Max had been glued to me since I had arrived home. He seemed to sense Celia was sick and was not his normal, rambunctious self.

While Celia slept, I called Sylvia to see if she could help take care of Celia while I was at work. She agreed she could stay with her every afternoon. Next, I contacted Gloria to ask her to change her hours at the store so I could spend each morning with

164

Celia. Gloria quickly agreed to open the store for me each morning and was glad she could help. Since that was set I made some vegetable soup that I thought Celia might be able to eat without too much trouble.

Just after four the phone rang and I jumped to grab it before it woke Celia. "Hello," I whispered.

"This is Officer Kast. I wanted to make you aware that we just raided the location where Roy was hiding out, but he managed to sneak out the back before we caught him."

"That's not good. If he's on foot he couldn't have gotten too far."

"That's what we were also hoping. We used a dog to track his scent, but unfortunately the dog lost him at the road's edge. That may mean he was picked up in a car. I'm concerned about Celia's safety. I've requested extra officers patrol your area just to make sure Roy doesn't try to finish what he started."

My gut was suddenly in a knot at the thought of having to possibly face Roy again. "Thanks for letting me know. Just in case you were wondering, the move to my house wore Celia out and she is resting, or I would let you talk to her yourself."

"Is it that obvious that I care about Celia?"

"Yes I want to warn you, though. Celia has had a very hard life. It may take a while before she will trust a man again. Don't get involved with her unless you're willing to stick it out for the long haul. I don't want my friend hurt any more."

"I totally understand. Don't worry, my intentions are honorable. I've got to run. Stay alert and keep your doors locked."

I smiled to myself that there was now someone in Celia's life that may finally treat her as she deserves. I looked up and Celia was standing in the doorway. "What are you doing out of bed?"

"I heard the phone ring. Is everything all right?"

I decided not to tell Celia about Roy still being on the run. She needed to concentrate on getting her strength back, and resting. "It was Calvin. He was just checking to see how you were doing."

"Well, that was sweet of him." Celia smiled.

Calvin may just be the best medicine to help Celia get her strength back. "Are you hungry? I made some soup."

"I'm still groggy from the pain pill and not particularly hungry. I know I need to eat. I'll try just a little."

I sat with Celia at the table while she sipped on her soup. "Sylvia is going to stop by after lunch tomorrow and keep you company while I work."

"She doesn't need to do that. I will be fine for a few hours alone."

"Nonsense. You need to learn that people enjoy helping you." Max suddenly jumped up and headed for the front door. "Harper must be home." As if on cue Harper opened the door to the pleasure of one happy dog.

"How was my boy today?" Harper asked as he roughed up Max, rubbing him from head to tail as Max danced around him.

I watched as Celia laughed. It was so good to see her smiling again. "That's what you need Celia, a dog to keep you company when you get well."

"I always wanted a dog. Do you think the women's shelter would let me have a small dog?"

"It never hurts to ask. Now that you have a steady job at the dealership you will probably be moving to your own place in a few months."

"Do you think I will still have a job after missing so many days at work?"

"You know they are dying to have you back at work. I am sure the paperwork is stacking up waiting for your return."

"I hope you're right. I guess I should call tomorrow and at least let them know when I might be able to return."

"Don't rush back too soon. Give your body a chance to heal."

I hugged and kissed Harper. "How was your day?"

166

"Busy. Since I took Monday off for our honeymoon, I've been playing catch up. I didn't have much time to eat lunch today. What did you have planned for supper?"

"My poor boy," I teased Harper and made a pouty face. "How does spaghetti sound?"

"I get no sympathy from my wife." To get me back for my comment he tickled my ribs.

Laughing, I pushed Harper away. "All right we are even. Supper will be ready in an hour."

"Why don't I take Max for a walk while you cook supper?" He leaned over and gave me a quick kiss before disappearing out the door with Max in the lead.

Celia sat in the kitchen with me while I cooked.

"You guys seem like the perfect couple," Celia said.

"I am very lucky to have found Harper. I can't imagine living my life without him. Maybe Calvin will make you as happy as Harper has made me."

"I can't even let myself think that. I've had so many disappointments in my life, I won't get my hopes up to be let down again."

I felt so bad for Celia. I knew it would take time for her to trust another man again. Harper and Max returned from their walk and brightened the mood in the room. Max ran, barking full of energy to his food dish. "If you ever get a dog be prepared for an additional food expense. Especially if you get a golden retriever with an appetite like Max's."

Celia laughed as she watched Max devour his meal in thirty-seconds flat. "That spaghetti smells awesome. It seems like forever since I had solid food."

"Do you want to try a little? It should be soft enough for you to chew."

"Sure, just give me a little, though, until I see how my stomach reacts to real food again."

After supper Celia indicated she was getting tired. "Thanks for supper. If you would excuse me I am going to head back to bed to rest some more."

"Don't hesitate to call me if you need anything."

After she closed the bedroom door I quietly motioned for Harper to follow me into the living room. I didn't want Celia overhearing my conversation. I explained to Harper that Roy was still on the run.

Harper was understandably upset. He walked around the house to make sure all the doors and windows were locked. "I don't want you taking Max out after dark. If he needs to go out I will take him," he firmly ordered.

I leaned over and kissed Harper gently on the lips to improve his mood. "I love you too."

He kissed me back. We were both tired and went to bed early. I couldn't sleep worrying about Roy being on the loose. Max seemed to sense my distress and nudged his wet nose against my face. I gently patted Max's head to let him know everything was okay. I finally fell asleep with my arm draped over Max and Harper's arms wrapped securely around me.

I woke with a start. Max was growling at the closed bedroom door. "Harper, wake up! Someone is in the house."

Harper reached into the night stand and pulled out his 9 mm handgun he now stored there. "You stay here. Keep Max with you and I will check it out."

I grabbed Max by the collar to keep him from running out of the room. I listened intently for the sound of an intruder. Then I heard a single gunshot. I leaped from the bed and ran down the hall. I saw the guest room door open where Celia was staying.

Harper yelled, "Call an ambulance." He was standing over Roy's body with the gun pointed at his head. Blood was pouring out of Roy's chest. Celia wasn't moving.

I frantically dialed 911 and yelled at the operator to send an ambulance. Before I had a chance to hang up the phone I could see the blue lights of a police cruiser outside the window. I opened the door and Calvin burst in.

"Is Celia hurt?" he yelled.

I directed him to the bedroom.

He walked in and took charge. He handcuffed Roy's hands behind his back even though he was in no shape to move. He rushed to Celia's side. "Celia, are you all right?" He grabbed her hand and felt for a pulse.

"Roy had a pillow over her face when I walked in," Harper said.

Celia's eyes started to blink and she sat up all of a sudden. "Celia, you're safe!" Calvin said. Celia started to sob. Calvin wrapped his strong arms around her, trying to comfort her. Calvin held her as her whole body shook with fear.

The house quickly filled with police and emergency personnel. Roy was taken away by ambulance with an armed guard to make sure he didn't escape again. Celia refused to go back to the hospital. She had just gotten out and didn't want to spend another hour there.

Celia gave her statement to the police. "I blacked out when a pillow was shoved over my face. When I regained consciousness Maggie and Calvin were by my side and Roy was on the floor by my bed."

Calvin, still by Celia's side, spoke up, "I know you're still recovering from your first attack. Are you sure you don't need to see a doctor?"

"Now that you have Roy in custody again I can rest easy which is all I need right now."

Calvin and I helped Celia to the sofa while the police crime scene unit did their job. They processed Celia's room and the kitchen, located in the back of the house, where Roy had broken a window to gain access inside. After what seemed like an eternity ,quiet fell over the house as everyone slowly left. The night had given way to morning. The sun now shined brightly through the window of the family room.

169

"Is anyone up for some strong coffee?" Still in my pajama's, which consisted of drawstring cotton shorts and a large t-shirt, I sat dazed while I waited for the coffeepot to stop gurgling.

Harper appeared in the kitchen all dressed for work. "Why don't you call in sick today? After last night I know you will be worthless at work."

"I am still the new guy at work and want to make a good impression. Since I took off for our honeymoon I can't afford to miss another day."

I handed him a cup of coffee in a travel mug. "Thanks for nailing a board over the hole in the window. I'll try to get someone here today to fix it." Harper kissed me quickly on the lips before racing out the door.

Celia came to life on the sofa. "Are you up for a little breakfast this morning?" I asked.

"Not really, but I know I've got to eat to get my strength back. How about I fix myself some runny oatmeal while you enjoy your coffee?"

Celia sat at the table with me and suddenly started to laugh. I thought she was losing it. "What is so funny?"

"You should see yourself in the mirror. Your hair is sticking straight up, you have two black eyes where your mascara ran and I think you have dog drool down the front of your t-shirt."

I looked at Celia with her face a pale yellow from the bruises, cast on her arm and tangled hair and realized what a sight we must behold. I started to laugh uncontrollably until tears came to my eyes. We were both laughing to keep down the hysteria of what we had just been through. "I needed that, thanks!" I leaned over and hugged Celia.

During breakfast Celia announced, "I think I should go back to the women's center now that Roy has been captured. I appreciate your hospitality but I would feel more comfortable in my own bed."

The guest room floor was covered in Roy's blood and the crime scene technicians had made a mess out of the room. They even took the pillow for evidence. I couldn't argue with Celia. "I understand. With the current state of my guest room you would probably feel more comfortable back at the woman's center. I'll help you gather your things after I take a much needed shower. I need to wash away my raccoon eyes," I laughed.

Just before noon I helped Celia get settled into her room at the women's center. I gave her some left over soup and spaghetti that she could easily heat in the microwave. She was joyously greeted by some of the other residents. When I left she was in good hands, with the other women vowing to watch over her.

"Call me if you need anything."

"Don't worry, I will be fine. I just need to sleep."

I hugged Celia and drove to my shop. This was my first day back to my store since my wedding, but it seemed like that was ages ago.

Gloria cheerfully greeted me. "How is the new Mrs. McGillian?"

"I am so glad to be back at work and returning to my normal routine. The last couple of weeks my emotions have been on a roller coaster. The shock of finding the limo driver dead after my bachelorette party, then the overwhelming happiness of getting married, then being terrified after finding out that Celia had been kidnapped, and finally my heart about broke when I first saw Celia near dead in the hospital. Oh, and you're never going to believe what happened last night. Roy broke into my house and tried to kill Celia again."

"Oh my word, is she all right?"

"Harper managed to shoot him before he succeeded in doing more harm to Celia."

"Did he kill him?"

"I know it's horrible for me to think, but I hope so. They took him to the hospital. This world would definitely be a better place without Roy in it, though. I hate the thought of Celia having to testify against him."

"You poor thing, you must be exhausted. Do you want me to stay this afternoon so you can get some rest?"

"No, I will be all right here with Max to keep me company." As if on cue Max laid across my feet. I bent down and patted him on the head. "My house is an absolute mess after the crime scene technicians did their thing. I really don't want to face the clean up just yet. Harper can help me scrub the floors and walls tonight when he gets home."

Gloria left and I sat peacefully in the shop until the phone rang. I looked at the caller ID. It was my mother. Crap, she probably heard through the grapevine about last night. I better answer it and take her verbal abuse rather than wait until later when it will even be worse. "Hello Mom, I was just about to call you," I lied.

"I just heard the police, with their blinding blue lights, were seen in front of your house last night. Are you okay?"

"I'm fine. Harper shot an intruder before he could hurt anyone." I was not ready to explain to Mom that the intruder was Roy, the guy who kidnapped me, just yet.

"Sweetie, I am worried about that neighborhood. It doesn't seem safe. Have you thought about selling your house and moving some place else?"

"No Mom, I am not going to sell my house. I need to get back to work."

"Before you run, do you think you could do your mother a favor and show up for supper Thursday night?"

"I know you haven't seen much of me since the wedding, but I've been kind of busy. I will try to make it to supper Thursday after work." The call ended. Mom once again guilted me into agreeing to come to supper on Thursday.

The rest of the day was uneventful, thankfully. By closing time I was about comatose I was so tired. I arrived home with Max, opened the door, and immediately was accosted by the mess that the crime scene technicians had left. I walked into the kitchen and realized I had also forgotten to call someone to fix the window. Max was full of energy, ready to eat and go for a walk. All I wanted to do was crawl into bed and sleep for a week.

Harper walked through the front door just as I started to feel totally overwhelmed at the enormity of the task in front of me. "I am so glad you're home! I know you must be tired, but can you take Max for a quick walk while I try to come up with something for supper?"

"I will do better than that." He held up a bag of Chinese food that he was hiding behind his back.

"My hero! Have I told you how wonderful you are today?" I hugged and kissed Harper. He wrapped his strong arms around my shoulders and all the worries of the day slipped away. My stomach started to growl and I realized I hadn't eaten since breakfast.

"The Chinese food smells awesome! I'll grab some plates and something to drink if you want to spread our feast out on the table."

I returned with sweet tea in hand and the table was full of an assortment of small white cartons. We filled our plates full with the delectable choices. "Oh, you remembered to get extra egg rolls, yum," I said as I crammed half a scrumptious egg roll in my mouth. We both ate until we were miserable.

"All I want to do now is to curl up with you in my arms and sleep," Harper said.

"Oh, that sounds so heavenly." Max's bark brought us out of our slumber. "I know you need to go out don't you boy?" Max responded with another bark. "Why don't you take Max for a short walk while I clean up the kitchen? Then we can find a good show on TV and forget about everything else until tomorrow."

"That sounds like a plan." Harper left with Max and I filled the dishwasher. I changed into shorts and a tank top and took charge of the remote control before Harper returned. I was channel surfing when Harper and Max came storming back into the house.

"No fair. I'm not in the mood for a chic flick tonight."

"You don't like my shows?" I teased, hiding the remote behind my back.

"You know what I mean. No romance shows tonight." He leaned down, kissed and tickled me playfully, grabbing the remote from me.

"I promise I will find something we both enjoy if you give me back the remote." I held out my hand and Harper surrendered the remote. I kissed him before he left to take a shower.

Harper quickly returned smelling of scented soap. He collapsed on the sofa next to me and wrapped his arm snugly around me. I rested my head against his chest. This was the first time we had relaxed together since our honeymoon. Unfortunately, we were both so exhausted and full from Chinese food, we fell sound asleep on the sofa within minutes.

# Nineteen

After a good night's rest I felt like a new person ready to face whatever challenges the day had in store for me. I arrived at the shop and it was not long before the phone rang. "Celia, I am so glad you called. How are you doing?"

"I am doing much better after sleeping about twelve hours. The reason I am calling though is Calvin just called."

"Oh really, did he ask you out?"

"Yes, but that's not why I called. Roy died in the hospital last night."

I tried to hide my joy at the news just in case it upset Celia that her ex-boyfriend was dead. "Really, I didn't realize his bullet wound was so serious."

"He made it through surgery, but had a stroke a few hours later. He died of a blood clot."

"Are you okay?"

"I don't know how I should feel. I cared for Roy before he turned violent. I know this sounds crazy but I truly believed he loved me."

"I'm sure Joanne has shared how abusers can have that affect over women. The abusive boyfriend or spouse thrives on controlling his partner. They tell you how much they care about you, but in reality the only way they know how to show their feelings is by hurting the ones they supposedly love."

"I know it's just one more chapter in my life closed."

"Exactly. Now tell me about Calvin. When are you going out with him? Do you think you may marry him one day?"

"Slow down! At least let me get through our first date before you start making wedding plans for me." Celia laughed.

"He just seems so nice. I want you to be happy. You deserve that out of life."

"Since I am in no shape to do much yet he asked if I would like to see a movie with him on Saturday."

"Wonderful, and I assume you said yes?"

"Of course. Do you think it's too soon to get involved with someone again after everything I went through with Roy?"

"You could use a healthy relationship to help you forget Roy and all the pain he caused you. I know I joked about you two getting married, but just have fun with no expectations. Just see where it goes."

Celia sounded more sure of herself now. "I guess you're right. What do I have to lose?"

"I want to hear all the details after your date." I looked up as Mom and Grandma walked through the door. "Unfortunately, I've got to run. I will talk to you later." I hung up the phone. "Hi, Mom. This is a surprise." I tried to sound pleased.

"I just wanted to stop by and remind you about supper tomorrow night."

"Yes Mom, Harper and I are planning to come over after work."

Grandma was casually browsing around the store while I talked to Mom. "Grandma, you know my inventory is getting kind of low. We need to hit some more garage sales."

"You know I was just thinking the same thing. The church is having its annual bazaar this Saturday starting at 8:00 AM. I bet you might find some treasures there."

I smiled to myself at Grandma's zest for finding a deal. "Why don't I pick you up at 7:45 so we don't miss out on anything?"

"You better make it 7:30. You know how all those church ladies like to grab up all the deals before anyone else can get to them."

I laughed at the thought that Grandma didn't consider herself one of those church ladies. Mom spoke up, "Well, your father will be home soon. We better run. I am making your favorite dessert for supper tomorrow," she added as she walked out the door.

She knew I couldn't resist her carrot cake. Mom always felt the best way to solve any problem was with food. I know she has been worried about me lately, but instead of letting me know how concerned she is, she showers me with food. It's Mom's way of telling me how much she loves me.

***

Supper at my parents' house is never dull. Mom likes to pry, but does it subtly. Grandma does not sensor any thoughts that come out of her mouth and will blurt out whatever is on her mind. Mom casually asked how we were adjusting to married life.

"Well, to be honest with you, between everything going on I haven't had much time to feel married yet. Harper and I haven't had much time to ourselves since our honeymoon. I don't think it has even set in that we are actually married yet." I smiled over at Harper hoping he would join the conversation.

Before he could say a word Grandma spoke up. "I bet your sex life is great with such a good looking fellow like Harper."

Mom turned beet red and was speechless. Dad pretended he didn't hear the question and quickly changed the subject to sports. "The Seminoles and Gators are playing a pre-season game this weekend. I happen to have three tickets. Would you and Harper like to attend the game with me?"

Harper spoke up for the first time since the meal began. "I would love to. You know I am a big Seminoles fan."

"I will have to pass. Grandma and I already made plans to go to the church bazaar Saturday morning then I need to work at the store until five. You guys go, though, and have fun." Dad finally had the son he dreamed of. I was thrilled to see Harper and Dad getting along so well. I think they had formed a special bond after working together to save me from Roy.

The evening was finally over. I showed Harper how appreciative I was for putting up with my family for the evening. We made passionate love and fell asleep in each other's arms.

***

Friday, the quilting club met after work. This was our first time getting together since my bachelorette party. Before work I stopped by the grocery store and picked up some wine, cheese, crackers, and of course a double chocolate cake I couldn't pass up. The day was busy with a steady stream of customers. It was a beautiful, hot August day in Florida and I think most of the customers were just trying to get out of the heat and enjoy the air conditioning.

Six o'clock finally came and I turned off the open sign. Gloria helped me set out the food and beverages. Audrey and Valerie car pooled and arrived first. They filled me in on how their kids were driving them nuts. They were overjoyed that school was starting back in session on Monday. Cynthia and Joanne arrived next. After hugs of joy, I poured everyone a glass of wine. Then a police car pulled up in front of the store. I stepped toward the door as my stomach tightened with dread. What purpose could they possibly have to stop by except to share more bad news? Then a smile came to my face as I watched Celia step out of the passenger side door.

"I am so glad you could make it!" I yelled. I opened the door for her and grabbed Celia's good arm and led her inside. "Look who I found!"

Everyone jumped to their feet and showered Celia in good wishes and hugs to welcome her back to the living.

"All right, ladies. Let's let Celia sit down before she collapses," Joanne said.

Celia laughed at all the attention. "I don't think I will be able to sew too much tonight, but I wanted to stop by and thank y'all for everything you did for me. Your cards and gifts along with the time you spent with me at the hospital meant more to me than you can imagine. You were instrumental in helping me regain my strength and recover from my injuries. I am truly blessed to have met such a wonderful group of women."

"I would like to make a toast." I poured Celia a glass of ginger ale since she was prohibited from drinking alcohol until her concussion had totally healed. Everyone held up their glasses. "To strong women and our friendship, which I will treasure forever."

Everyone yelled, "Cheers!" We all clicked our glasses together and took a sip.

Joanne spoke up, "Where is Sylvia?"

"I talked to her last night and she was planning to attend. She must be running late." Before I could say another word I heard the bell on the front door ring. I glanced up to see who it was. Sylvia walked in with her arms full of presents.

"What is all this?" I asked as I helped place the presents on the table.

"These are the presents from you bachelorette party. The Orlando police contacted me yesterday to let me know the presents were being released from evidence. I was told I could pick them up. So here they are."

"These are the presents that were in the trunk with the dead limo driver?" Cynthia asked with a disgusted look on her face.

"Yes, but don't worry they're clean. The police found no DNA evidence on them."

Celia spoke up, "Did they tell you who killed the limo driver?"

I knew Celia was still thinking that Roy may have had something to do with it.

"Yes, they did. The police discovered the limo driver's girlfriend had a very jealous ex-boyfriend. The police found DNA evidence on the limo driver which connected the ex-boyfriend to the murder."

"That shows you what power we women have over our men!" Audrey joked to lighten the mood.

We laughed the night away, sewing very little, but enjoyed each others company. Gloria  caught us up on all the latest rumors around town. As the night went on, now tipsy from the wine, I opened my bachelorette presents and blushed as I held up the lingerie. "This looks to be more for Harper's enjoyment than mine," I laughed. It was so risqué it left nothing to the imagination.

***

Saturday morning arrived and I picked Grandma up at 7:30AM as promised. It was a warm August day. I pulled back my hair in a ponytail and wore a cool sundress to ward off the heat and humidity. I drove up to my parents' house to find Grandma waiting for me on the front porch. She was eager to arrive at the church bizarre to find the deal of the day. As soon as I stopped the car in the church parking area and before I could even turn off the engine, Grandma jumped out and rushed towards the tables with their merchandise displayed. The front lawn of the church was lined with at least fifty tables selling everything from food to crafts, and all kinds of knick knacks. I made my way down the aisle and suddenly stopped. There was my dog biscuit jar where I had hidden the Spanish coins. I quickly grabbed the jar and opened it. I peered inside and found it empty. "Do you know who donated this item to the sale?" I asked the lady behind the table.

"No, I am afraid not. We have been collecting items for almost six months."

I was resolved to the fact that the coins were gone. For nostalgic reasons I decided to buy back the brightly colored jar. After finding a few more items I thought I could sell at my store, I headed to the car. Grandma was waiting for me in the shade with her purchase by her feet. It was a large swordfish. It was plastic and brightly painted to look like a real swordfish.

"Grandma, what are you doing with that swordfish?"

"You know how much your Dad likes to fish. I bought it for him. It was a steal at five dollars."

I knew exactly what Dad would think of the swordfish and it was not good thoughts. "Don't you think it might be a little big to fit in the house?"

"He can hang it at his boat repair shop. I see you found the jar I donated for you."

All the color drained from my face.

Grandma continued, "While you were on your honeymoon, your Mom and I stopped by your house to pick up some more food for Max. I saw this pretty painted jar on the shelf in your utility room. It didn't look like it was being used for anything so I donated it for you."

I tried to remain calm and spoke slowly. "Grandma, what did you do with the coins that were inside?"

"Oh, you mean the rusted pieces of metal I found inside? I was going to throw them away."

I held my breath as she continued.

"I decided you might want them, though, and left them on my dresser. I meant to give them to you when you were at the house for supper the other night, but forgot."

A big smile came across my face. "Grandma, have I told you how much I love you recently?"

She puffed out her chest as if I had just given her an award.

"Thank you for holding onto those rusted pieces of metal for me."

"Don't let me forget to give them to you when we get home."

I attempted to load Grandma's plastic swordfish into the back seat of the car. It was too long to fit. I had to open the sun roof and let the sword portion stick through the opening. On our drive home I received many strange looks from people passing my car. Thank goodness Dad and Harper had already left for the football game when I arrived. I quickly hid the swordfish in the garage before Mom saw it. I followed Grandma in the house.

"Hi dear, did you find any new treasures for your store?" Mom asked.

"Yes, as a matter of fact I did. Grandma is justing retrieving something off her dresser for me, then I have to run to open the store." I stared at Grandma and she suddenly remembered about the coins. She headed toward her bedroom while I anxiously waited for her to return.

"Can I get you some breakfast before you leave?"

"No, I don't have time. I am running late as it is," I explained.

"Here you go," Grandma said as she handed me the burlap bag with the coins.

I peered inside the bag, unable to believe my eyes, all the coins were there. "Thanks Grandma, I'll see you at church tomorrow," I added as I rushed out the door.

I dialed Harper's cell phone when I reached my car. As soon as he answered I blurted out, "I found the coins. I don't have time to explain right now but will share with you tonight." I placed the coins back in the jar and didn't let them out of my sight all day long.

# Twenty

Harper and I decided to donate the coins in Herman and Dorothy's name to the Putnam County Historical Society. Several weeks later a big dedication ceremony was held to officially celebrate the lives of Herman and Dorothy Evanston and their generous contribution to the society. I was asked to speak on their behalf. At first, I didn't have a clue what I would say. I knew so very little about them. But then I realized I knew more than I thought.

The night of the ceremony arrived. I was surprised by the large turn out. The president of the Historical Society stood up to speak and everyone found their seats and a hush came over the room. He began by thanking everyone for attending. He gave a brief introduction and motioned for me to come to the podium to speak.

I was suddenly very nervous as everyone's attention was directed at me. I swallowed deeply to clear my throat. "Thank you so much for having such a beautiful ceremony to honor Herman and Dorothy Evanston. They were a vital part of this community for over thirty years. During the refurbishment of their home I learned about their lives and what they meant to this community. Along with talking to my neighbors and people who knew them, I discovered they were very special people. I am very sorry I never had the opportunity to meet them in person myself. Herman was a hard working honest man. When he found the coins while clearing some land many years ago, he didn't want to boast about his find. Instead, he hid the coins in his house, I'm sure with intent to do something with them later. It was fortunate for me that later came after he and Dorothy passed away. As you know, Dorothy and Herman both passed away suddenly. Herman from heart trouble and Dorothy from an intruder." Soft whispers arose from the audience as I spoke. "I am sure due to Dorothy's untimely demise she didn't have time to share the coins before she passed. Just by luck Harper and I found the container doing yard work one day." I didn't stretch the truth too much and left out the role that Dorothy's ghost had played in finding the coins. "After much consideration, Harper and I knew that the coins rightly belonged to this community to be shared and enjoyed. So today I am here to dedicate the coins in Herman and Dorothy's name so that they may be remembered forever."

I received a standing ovation from the attendees. Everyone was so grateful for the donation.

*** 

Things slowly returned to normal, well as normal as life can be for me. For Christmas I gave Harper the best present of all by announcing I was pregnant. Being with child didn't slow me down much. I had a very easy pregnancy. Mom hovered over me like a hawk making sure I ate right and took care of myself. I worked up to the day I went into labor. My water broke while I was helping a customer check out. Thank goodness I was behind the counter when it happened. Gloria was there with me and calmly took charge, calling Harper at work to tell him I was in labor. While I waited for Harper to arrive I changed into the spare clothes I kept at the store. To my surprise and relief, I went into labor a week early. Instead of having the baby around August sixth as planned he was born July twenty-eighth, the same day my Dad was born. He finally had the son he always wanted by having a grandson to spoil and teach how to fish and hunt.

Max loved the new addition to our family. He jumped up every time the baby cried, to retrieve one of his toys. He would drop a toy in the bassinet, trying to console the baby and stop the crying and tears. Surprisingly enough it worked, sometimes turning the tears to giggles when Max nudged the toy in the baby's hands, placing his wet nose against his tear moistened face.

184

Celia fully recovered from her injuries. She had a quick romance with Calvin and they were married in the fall, the week after Thanksgiving. They knew right away that they were meant to be together just like Harper and I. They didn't want to delay spending the rest of their lives together. Celia became pregnant shortly after I did and gave birth the first week in September. She also had a boy, to Calvin's delight. I was thrilled at the thought of our sons growing up together and hopefully being best friends like us.

There were no more ghost sightings and I hoped that Dorothy was now resting peacefully after guiding me to her hidden secrets.

Grandma's constant desire to go to garage sales has kept my store well supplied with treasures and more for years to come.

## About The Author

Diane E. Izzard lives in Welaka, Florida near the St. Johns River. The laid back Florida life style provides her the inspiration she needs to write. She has a bachelor degree in Industrial Engineering and master degree in Management. She worked at Kennedy Space Center until 2013 when she started her writing career. She loves dogs, hiking, biking, skiing, and curling up with a good book. Her latest dog, an Alaskan Malamute, provides the personality for the dogs in her stories. Visit her on Facebook at www.facebook.com/Dianee.Izzard.